Such A Dirty Game...

A Novel by
Chauncy Starling

PAGE PUBLISHING, INC.
Conneaut Lake, PA

First originally published by Page Publishing 2021

ISBN 978-1-64544-574-6 (pbk)
ISBN 978-1-64544-575-3 (digital)

Printed in the United States of America

Chapter 1

It was the winter of 1994 on a dark frigid night in the merciless and eerie streets of Wilmington, Delaware. Abdullah, a caramel-complexioned teenager in his late teens, stood in a lightless alleyway that was surrounded by row homes in between Twenty-Third Street and Twenty-Fourth Street, hiding from the badges that were patrolling the area for any illegal activities.

"Yo, Ab, he want ten dimes," Dusty announced as he entered the alley and was accompanied by a crack addict, directing him toward the five-footer Abdullah. Quickly, Abdullah drew a sandwich bag from his pocket that contained rocks, artfully handing the stones to the crack fiend who exchanged dead presidents.

"Can I get mine?"

"I just brought you a hundred-dollar sale," Dusty proclaimed.

"A yo, stop playing with me," Abdullah said sternly, whipping out a .45 Desert Eagle semiautomatic, pressing the cannon against Dusty's chest. "I said five sales, not three. You only brought three. This ain't the eighties when you was eating good calling the shots. Those days are long gone blown in the wind. You're a crackhead now without a pot to piss in."

Defenselessly, and helplessly, Dusty huffed, while Abdullah withdrew his firearm from his chest.

Peering out of the alley, Dusty observed junkies marching up the street. Energetically, Dusty flagged the crack fiends down. "Yo! Right here my peoples got dat butter."

Abdullah made the crack sale, and then he made another.

"Young nigga, get me, me!" Dusty said excitedly.

"Here, man," Abdullah said as he handed Dusty a rock.

"I'll be back," Dusty said with bugged eyes, disappearing into the darkness, clutching his street candy as if he were a thief in the night yearning and heading to smoke the little stone he grasped.

Abdullah's pager exploded: *Beep, beep, beep.* He reached for his loot clocker, snatching it off his hip, examining the screen that displayed "2-4."

Immediately, Abdullah knew who it was because 2-4 was the code his friend used. Pretty, the six-foot, dark-coffee-complexioned twenty-year-old was from Twenty-Fourth and Lamotte Street. The same block Boom-Bam ran up and down devouring its riches. Abdullah frequented Twenty-Second and Carter Street where Poohmier was from. Boom-Bam and Poohmier were ghetto stars, street legends known for their trigger happiness and known for their knack to gobble up dead presidents. Arguably, they were among the most notorious thugs that the city of Wilmington had ever seen.

Abdullah strolled to a pay phone that was located on Twenty-Fourth and Market Street, slamming twenty-five cents into the talk machine that sat on the side of a Chinese eatery. The telephone rang twice.

"Yo!" Pretty answered.

"What's up, Dog?" Abdullah replied, looking around the streets and surveying the hood, only to discover two lawmen glaring, sitting in a squad car at the intersection waiting on the streetlight.

"Where you at, Ab?" Pretty queried.

"I'm in front of the Chinese store. I'm at Chad's. One Time is at the light hawking me," Abdullah relayed, glancing at the police.

Meanwhile, the streetlight switched green while the lawmen hesitatingly eased through the intersection with their eyes fixed on Abdullah.

"Ab, come down Brooke's," Pretty said.

Brooke was Pretty's girl, his world. He was deeply in love with her, no doubt, head over heels. She stayed down on Concord Avenue blocks away.

"I'm coming right now. It's hot out here, the block is hot. I'm out," Abdullah replied.

Just as Abdullah placed the receiver back on its hook, a '90 dark-blue Buick Riviera carrying menacing figures with dark hoodies crept down Market Street.

Immediately, under pressure, Abdullah grabbed his pistol, sliding his finger on the trigger as his heart shook with anxiety as if it was about to burst out of his chest. With his eyes glued on the mysterious car, with his finger ready to squeeze the trigger in case the menacing figures with dark hoodies drew their lethal weapons, Abdullah carefully observed the shady vehicle glide down the strip, vanishing into the somberness of the bleak ghetto.

Will I see twenty-one? Abdullah thought to himself as he proceeded to Brooke's.

While Abdullah toed down Market Street underneath the pale sparkly streetlights, he reflected back to when he was thirteen years old.

Summertime, 1988, on a bright scalding day in Chester County, Pennsylvania.

"Abdullah, come eat your food. It's getting cold! Come and get it!" Abdullah's grandmother shouted.

"Here I come, Mom Mom," Abdullah replied, making his way into the dining room to find his grandmother sitting comfortably at the dining room table.

"Uncle Bilal will be by tomorrow to take you to Jumuah," Abdullah's grandmother said softly.

As Abdullah sat with his grandmother, eating her remarkable fried chicken, the telephone rang out. Abdullah's grandmother grabbed the telephone from the table. "Hello?" she sang into the receiver.

"Hello. Can I speak to Abdullah?"

"Yes, you can, who is this?" Abdullah's grandmother fired back.

"Tim," he said.

"Hold on," she said, handing her grandson the telephone. "It's the boy from next door."

"Hello?" Abdullah said calmly.

"What's up, Abdullah? You coming outside?" Tim replied.

"Yeah, I'll be out," Abdullah answered.

Twenty minutes later Abdullah and his friend Tim idled in front of his grandmother's house.

"Abdullah, I got something I wanna show you, but you can't tell nobody, and I mean nobody. You gotta keep this a secret," Tim said earnestly, displaying a serious facial expression. "Come on, I'll show you," he added.

While the two youngsters coasted through the streets of Pennsylvania, Abdullah's mind raced. *What's the secret? Could it be a stolen car? A stolen bike? What could it be?* The suspense was racking his brain.

The young bucks journeyed across fields and hills, eventually coming upon a run down graveyard. As they proceeded through the cemetery, they saw the tombstone of Sydnor Doman. Sydnor Doman was murdered the summer before for turning state witness on a liquor-store stickup. His own friends carried out the deed. It was crazy how they killed him. They unrighteously and ruthlessly held him down and injected him with heroin. The kind that was as pure as a virgin. On a mellow night, lawmen found Sydnor Doman cold as ice, dead, laid out on the pavement with syringes hanging out of his eyes and arms.

"Dat was my bol Sydnor Doman. I miss that nigga," Tim said with sympathy looming in his eyes.

"Yo! How the hell are you gonna have love for a snitch? If you was the one who stuck the liquor store up, he would have told on you too. Fuck him," Abdullah barked.

Abdullah and his friend Tim made their way back to the end of the ill-favored cemetery.

"How far do we gotta go?" Abdullah asked.

"Right up there in them woods," Tim replied, pointing toward the island mass of trees, bushes, and plants.

As they entered the woods, Tim glanced at Abdullah and quickly said, "Ain't no turning back now."

The young bucks moved through the woods in complete silence, not one word was uttered. Then all of a sudden there it was. Abdullah's eyes bulged, his heart dropped. The stench of something foul and unbearable to sniff filled the air. There lay a man with his eyes open with flies lingering around him, displaying a hole the size of a dime in his head.

Fighting off the urge of vomiting from the horrendous smell of death, Abdullah stared at the dead man in amazement. The lifeless man clutched a silver firearm as if he was in a gun battle and lost or simply was beaten to the draw.

"Look, he's got a gat in his hand," Tim exclaimed.

The second after Tim spoke, Abdullah reached over the corpse, recklessly seizing the lethal weapon.

"See if he got any dough on him," Abdullah directed.

At first Tim hesitated to search the lifeless body, but he proceeded to shake down the corpse. As Tim rifled through the dead man's pocket, he discovered a knot of dead presidents, and he swiftly counted the paper while Abdullah looked on from the sideline.

"We got five hundred!" Tim declared hysterically, pausing upon noticing Abdullah's icy facial expression. "Why are you looking at me like that?"

Abdullah took a deep breath. "Tim, give me the dough and I mean all of it."

Uncontrollably, Abdullah's hand shook as he slowly lifted the silver lethal weapon, leveling it at Tim's forehead.

"Abdullah! Abdullah! What are you doing? No! Noo!"

Before Tim knew what hit him, a slug flew clean into his skull, killing him instantly.

*****

Abdullah climbed up the steps to Brooke's row house and knocked on the front door.

"Who is it?" a sweet, tiny voice answered.

"It's Abdullah," he said confidently.

The door swung open, and there stood Brooke. Her face was very pleasing, occupying a mahogany complexion accompanied by jet-black wavy hair flowing down her back with a body that exhibited alluring features.

"Pretty, your boy Abdullah is here!" Brooke yelled at the top of her lungs, while she invited Abdullah into her house.

"What's up, Ab?" Pretty said as he greeted his friend with a handshake and a hug.

"Where my girl at?" Abdullah inquired, scanning the living room.

"She's still out New Castle waiting for you to call her. I know she paged you, didn't she?" Brooke replied.

Slightly smiling, Abdullah nodded, falling on to the couch that furnished the living room, grabbing a cordless telephone from a nearby table, promptly drumming the numbers.

"Hello?" a voice that was similar to Brooke's but not as sweet as hers answered.

"Hello?" Abdullah fired back.

"Who is this?" she fired back.

"Girl, stop playing. It's your boo," Abdullah retorted.

"Why the hell haven't you called me all day? Boy, I've been paging your ass all day. Where are you at?" she said.

"I'm at your cousin's. You coming in town?" Abdullah said.

"You know I am. Abdullah, are you gonna get my nails done?" she replied.

"Monifah, I don't be doing that kind of shit. I got you, though. I want my name on your nails too," Abdullah fired back.

"Abdullah, do you love me?" Monifah questioned softly.

"You know I do," Abdullah asserted.

"Well, it shouldn't be a problem with you getting my nails done. It shouldn't be. I don't be doing that kind of shit. It should be 'Yes, baby, I'll get your nails done. I know you're a thug and everything, "but when you're with me you don't got to be that. I'll be in town in an hour. All right, baby? I love you," Monifah expounded.

"I love you too," Abdullah followed.

"All right bye. Hang up, Ab," Monifah said, smiling ear to ear.

"No, you hang up first," Abdullah fired back.

Reluctantly, Abdullah hung up, and then Monifah followed suit.

"I love you. I love you too. You all in love with Monifah, ain't you? You hang up. No, you hang up. No, you hang up first," Pretty teased.

"Man, I ain't in love," Abdullah contested, lying through his teeth.

"Ab, Monifah said she loved you, and you told her you loved her. You didn't even want to get off the phone with her. I mean y'all both didn't even want to hang up. You're not in love? I hear you," Pretty said as he laughed, making a facial expression that read "yeah right."

"Pretty, it's on tonight. I got a caper. You down? It's bout fifteen pounds," Abdullah said with a baleful smile.

"Who you talking about getting?" Pretty inquired with a suspicious frown.

"The cat I be copping my weed from! The Jamaican," Abdullah relayed.

"Shyba? Nigga, is you crazy? He'll murder you. You know that Jamaican got bodies. He ain't to be fucked with, I'm telling you. Ab, you gotta chill with robbing motherfuckers. I'm saying you can't even walk down the block without watching your back, 'cuz all the niggas you done robbed. I can't live like that. I'm saying you don't gotta jack nobody. I'm getting money, you're getting money. So why keep doing it? Risking the chances of getting knocked for a robbery rap. That's two to twenty or getting killed. Listen, after tonight, after you handle your business, after you off the weed, your change will be right. I got a connect down Florida. Twenty geez for a key, and they'll front you a key. When we come back from that trip, ain't no looking back. Let them old ways go, kill the jacking shit," Pretty said sincerely as he gave Abdullah a firm hand shake, looking him directly in his eyes.

Two hours later, Monifah stood outside on the doorstep of Brooke's row home, eagerly tapping on the front door. Monifah possessed a rich, dark-chocolate complexion associated with a lovely face that held a warm smile. Her locks were short and neatly cropped, the exact same style that Toni Braxton sported at that particular time. She flaunted a stop-traffic, car-accident figure.

In a matter of minutes, the door swung open, revealing a beaming Brooke.

Monifah returned a smile and strolled into the house to find Abdullah sitting in the living room, watching her as if he were a hawk, watching her every move. Their eyes locked as she exhaled deeply from the slight shyness that consumed her.

Damn, she the shit. I can't wait to beat that virgin pussy to death, Abdullah thought to himself while Monifah approached.

"What's up, Ab? You miss me?" Monifah said energetically, smiling innocently, flopping onto the couch right next to Abdullah.

Moments later, Abdullah's pager erupted. Immediately, he drew his loot clocker from his pocket, peering at the beeper's screen.

"Yo, I gotta use the horn." Abdullah commenced to drumming the numbers on the cordless telephone. Once Abdullah departed the row house, closing the door behind him, he looked back carefully and slyly, making sure that Monifah was out of ear distance as he slowly toed down the steps.

"Somebody page Abdullah?" he questioned.

"Yeah it's your girl Sami! You know it. What's the deally?" she exclaimed.

"Ain't shit," Abdullah fired back.

"I'm trying to smoke some trees and get my pussy knocked from the back. I need to taste some dick. Word I do," Sami said candidly.

"Where you at?" Abdullah pried.

"I'm on market, 2-9. Let's get a room," Sami replied.

"All right, give me a minute. Are you gonna be at this number?" Abdullah said hurriedly.

"Yeah, just don't take all day," Sami said.

"Bet, I'm hit you back in a minute," Abdullah said, disconnecting the cordless telephone.

Abdullah stepped back into Brooke's house to find Monifah sitting patiently and quietly on the couch.

Abdullah sighed and walked up to Monifah. "Mo, baby, I'm gonna make this sale real quick, then get us something to eat," he said calmly.

"Oh no you're not. You're not going anywhere. I came in town to be with you, to get my quality time. Everything can wait. Your drug dealing can wait. Everything can wait. I'm your priority, and you're my priority right now. Understand?" Monifah said firmly, rising from the couch, peering deep into Abdullah's eyes, grabbing him gently, and pressing her lips against his.

"All right, Mo, I'm chilling. But later on I gotta get this cheddar," Abdullah replied.

"Why do you carry a gun?" Monifah asked in a childlike manner, feeling the firearm that rested in Abdullah's waistband.

"For protection, baby girl. You know from the stickup bol's that be trying to jack a nigga," Abdullah said solemnly.

"What is it?" Abdullah inquired with a puzzled-facial expression, reading the discomfort in his girlfriend's body language.

"You're not gonna be out all night? Are you?" Monifah questioned.

"Nah I won't be out long," Abdullah answered.

Drinking Hennessy straight out of the bottle, Abdullah pondered on his fate. Would he die pulling the caper?

As it got late, Abdullah prepared to make his move. Win, lose, or draw things were about to get extremely ugly. Fright night polluted his mind, and he was determined—headstrong—to carry it out.

Animatedly, Abdullah drummed the numbers to the cordless telephone. Ring Ring. Swiftly, Monifah snatched the phone up.

"Hello?" she sang into the receiver.

"Somebody just page Shyba from there?" he inquired.

"Yeah hold on," Monifah said, passing the cordless telephone to her boyfriend. "Ab, it's for you."

"Yo, I'm ready," Abdullah declared.

"Where you at?" Shyba queried.

"I'm over the north side," Abdullah relayed.

"Come over west side. I'm at the spot," Shyba said with a thick Jamaican accent.

"All right, dog," Abdullah said calmly.

Click! They hung up.

"Mo, call the cab for me so I can get this cheddar," Abdullah said smoothly, handing his girlfriend the cordless telephone.

"You're not gonna drive your car?" Monifah pried with a puzzled facial expression.

"Nah," Abdullah said plainly.

Moments later, a cab pulled up in front of Brooke's row house, blaring its horn.

"Abdullah, your ride is out front," Monifah informed, as her eyes peered out of the window, landing on the yellow cab, then across the street on Abdullah's '85 black beat-up Chevrolet Impala. Subsequently turning to face her boyfriend, she said, "Be safe."

"Don't worry. I'll be back. Don't go to sleep, all right?" Abdullah said while he headed to the front door, departing the row home.

"I love you!" Monifah shouted to Abdullah, as he made his way down the steps to the waiting cab.

Just before Abdullah climbed into the waiting taxi, he looked back at Monifah as if he would never ever see her again, while she stood calmly in the doorway.

"Where are you going, slick?" the middle-aged man with ivory complexion asked while he turned the meter on, pulling off with ease.

Minutes later, just as the cab driver came upon the block where the building of the Department of Motor Vehicles stood, Abdullah abruptly announced, "All right right here" while he whipped out a large knot of dead presidents that consisted of hundreds, fifties, twenties, tens, fives, proceeding to pay the taximan.

Blocks away from the Department of Motor Vehicles, Abdullah strolled up to a house in a working-class neighborhood. Before knocking on the front door, Abdullah took out his .45 Desert Eagle semiautomatic and switched off the safety.

"Who is it?" a lady's voice answered.

"It's Abdullah," he said.

"Come in," the woman directed.

Abdullah entered the lush home, making his way through the hallway, stepping into the living room to find a lady with a yellowish complexion with intense beauty.

"Hey, Abdullah," she greeted.

"What's up, Coco?" Abdullah replied.

"My husband will be down in a sec. Have a seat," Coco said as she flopped into a love seat comfortably, switching the television channel with the remote.

As Abdullah and Coco scoped the idiot box, Shyba breezed into the living room, toting a huge duffel bag that bulged with marijuana.

"You ready to get this paper, young 'un?" Shyba said, encountering Abdullah.

"I ain't got time for bitches, gotta keep my mind on my ritches," Abdullah retorted, reciting a hook from Tupac Shakur's *Thug Life: Volume 1.*

"It's nineteen pounds of that sticky in here. That bomb shit, mon," Shyba proclaimed, glancing at the duffel bag. From out of the blue suddenly, Abdullah commenced to laugh vilely, and simultaneously Shyba and Coco peered at one another, exhibiting facial expressions that read, "What the hell is he laughing at?" Then the married couple reverted their attention back on Abdullah.

Still laughing, Abdullah eagerly climbed out of his seat, producing his .45 Desert Eagle semiautomatic. Abdullah gestured for Shyba to have a seat using his firearm as a warning, and without any hesitation Shyba complied. "You know what it is. Run that shit," Abdullah ranted, as his laughter ceased and his face became cold as ice.

"Okay, mon. Okay, mon. Just don't shoot," Shyba entreated pathetically, holding his hands in the air.

"Please don't kill us, please!" Coco screamed in dread, while tears raced down her face.

"Shut the fuck up, bitch! I ain't trying to hear that shit. Where the cheddar at?" Abdullah barked heartlessly.

"Ab, you like fam. Why is you doing this? I watched you grow up with my little brother and little cousin. When you ran away from home you stayed with my people. They took you in. This ain't right," Shyba said persuasively, trying to play on Abdullah's conscience, as he nervously pushed the huge duffel bag with his foot toward the armed Abdullah.

"Where's the cheddar, Shyba? I ain't playing," Abdullah exclaimed.

"It's in the back room, in the safe," Shyba informed. "It's nuffin but seven geez in there. I don't keep that much here."

"Yeah, I know you don't keep all your cheddar here, you would be a dumb motherfucker if you did. Your change is probably in the bank somewhere. Or buried somewhere, or at another crib. That ain't my concern, though. I don't give a fuck about that. My concern is right here, right now," Abdullah fired back.

With Abdullah brandishing his lethal weapon at the heads of the married couple, they timidly and slowly led him into the back-room. Once in the back room held at gunpoint by Abdullah, who stared flagrantly, Shyba removed a picture frame from off the wall, revealing a safe.

"What the hell are you waiting for? Open that shit. Don't play with me. I'm telling you," Abdullah growled.

Terror gripped Coco's being immensely as she watched Abdullah carry out his devious plan while Shyba's hands shook ungovernably, twisting the knob to the safe. In a matter of seconds, the door to the safe swung open. And with that, Abdullah smiled ear to ear.

With a blink of an eye, Abdullah fired a bullet into the middle of Shyba's forehead, spattering his blood and brains onto the wall as he slid down the wall, breathless.

"No, no, oh my God! You killed Shyba!" Coco howled with dread and tears in the windows of her eyes. "Please, please. I'll do anything you want, just let me live. Please."

"Is that right?" Abdullah said tauntingly, accompanied with a crooked smile.

"Yes, anything. Please!" Coco whined.

"Anything?" Abdullah replied as he rubbed the barrel of his firearm against Coco's love box. "Take off your pants for me."

Crying hysterically and shaking violently, Coco proceeded to unfasten her jeans, sliding them down to her thighs.

"Pull your pants back up. Fucking you would be my downfall. I am a lot of things, but I ain't a rapist. I'll let you live, but if you try some hoe shit, I'll kill your moms and your whole family. Right now you're gonna walk me to the pay phone. Come on, let's go," Abdullah said coldly.

As Coco walked with Abdullah to the telephone booth, she wondered if Abdullah would kill her. She grasped a little hope. After all, she was still inhaling the air of the world. Coco kind of figured that Abdullah didn't really want to slay her due to the fact that the opportunity presented itself, and he didn't engage in the horrible deed. Although Coco knew what Abdullah was capable of after seeing firsthand Shyba's brains plastered on the wall.

The vision of her husband catching a slug to the head haunted her mind, and she would do absolutely anything not to die like that.

Standing at the telephone booth, Abdullah and Coco, Abdullah paged Pretty. Five minutes later, Pretty responded.

"Yo!" Abdullah said calmly.

"Where you at? Monifah is waiting," Pretty replied.

"Come get me on some ol. I'll be at the DMV," Abdullah said, eyeing Coco.

"All right, dog, I'm on my way," Pretty fired back.

Click! The friends hung up.

*****

Moments later, Abdullah and Coco entered her residence. They stepped to the back room, immediately landing their eyes on Shyba, his back leaning against the wall, while he sat on the floor lifeless with his eyes wide open. Coco exploded with tears; just seeing the love of her life in that state shattered her into pieces.

"Yo put the cheddar in the fucking bag," Abdullah commanded.

Quickly, Coco placed the dead presidents into the bag, wiping her tears with her left hand. She pondered about her fate.

Will I survive the clutches of this madman? Coco thought to herself, sobbing.

"Stop, stop crying. You're my girl now. Ain't that right?" Abdullah said grinning.

Coco sighed with unhappiness in her eyes. "Yes, Abdullah, I'm your girl now. It's done, that's all the money."

"Listen, you can't tell nobody about this. Remember our deal. If you try to do some bullshit, you'll be wearing a black dress at your mom's funeral," Abdullah said sternly.

"Thank you, Abdullah," Coco replied as her voice cracked with emotion.

"I'm out," Abdullah said, making his way to the front door, turning his back on Coco, and proceeding to exit the house.

At the front door, Abdullah stopped in his tracks, dropping the blood money that was held in a paper bag, also, releasing the huge duffel bag that contained the marijuana that led to Shyba's demise.

Smiling cunningly, Abdullah darted back to the back room to be greeted by a weeping Coco, who rested her head on her husband's chest.

Coco felt eyes ripping her face apart. She looked up, and unexpectedly to her, there stood Abdullah displaying a monstrous facial expression. Trembling uncontrollably, shedding tears profusely, Coco slowly rose to her feet. Abdullah simply peered into Coco's eyes for a minute. Then he swiftly leveled his firearm at Coco's head. Before she could let out a scream, a slug penetrated her skull. Coco perished in the same manner as Shyba, one to the brain.

Aloofly, Abdullah grasped the huge duffel bag and paper bag, striding out of the house as if he were a law-abiding citizen.

Minutes later, Abdullah arrived at the Department of Motor Vehicles where Pretty sat calmly in his rimmed-up white Toyota Corolla 1.8 (lowrider).

Abdullah climbed into the lowrider. "Yo! get the fuck away from here," he said with a serious facial expression.

"I see you," Pretty replied smiling, viewing the huge duffel bag and paper bag.

Abdullah nodded to his friend.

As Abdullah and Pretty shot through Wilmington, from out of nowhere—from the woodwork of the dark streets—there emerged a squad car pulling alongside the lowrider.

"Oh shit. One Time is on the side of us," Pretty informed. "Don't look, nigga."

Artfully, the squad car dropped back and switched lanes, easing behind the hoodlums, as if they were on the verge of pulling them over.

"Now they behind us," Pretty exclaimed worriedly, stalking the rearview mirror with popped eyes.

"Nigga, just drive like they ain't behind us. If it come down to it, it's a high-speed chase, dat all. You know how we do," Abdullah expounded.

Street after street, after street, after street, the lawmen trailed the lawbreakers on their heels.

Still staring into the rearview mirror, Pretty observed the driver of the squad car jump onto the radio while his partner read the lowrider's license plate.

"The pig's on his radio," Pretty said excitedly.

"He might be calling for backup," Abdullah replied.

"I'm ready to take them for a ride. "Fuck dat! Hold on."

"It's getting ready to be on," Pretty said, with a cockiness in his voice.

"Chill, let's wait till they flash their lights," Abdullah suggested.

Heart pounding like a drum, Abdullah clutched his .45 Desert Eagle semiautomatic, exhaling deeply, taking the firearm off safety. "It's whatever. It's nuffin, they ain't God. I'll send them to God, you hear me?"

Seconds after Abdullah's declaration, the badges turned off, heading for another direction.

"They don't want it!" Abdullah ranted.

"Dat was a close one. I'm telling you, Ab. Damn dat was a close one," Pretty said, relieved, sighing.

"Them punk-ass cops followed us from the west side to the north side," Abdullah said with irritation in his voice.

Moments later, Abdullah and his friend Pretty pulled up to Brooke's row home. Pretty cut off the engine as a beaming Monifah appeared at the doorway.

Abdullah and Pretty climbed out of the rimmed-up white lowrider.

"What's up, baby?" Monifah greeted Abdullah energetically, while she let him and Pretty into the row house.

Once inside of the dwelling, Abdullah bear-hugged Monifah as Teena Marie's "Out on a Limb" played and floated in the backdrop.

"I told you I will be back. I wouldn't be long," Abdullah said smoothly, with his arm roped around Monifah.

"Ab, I'll holla at you later on," Pretty said as he proceeded to make his way up the stairs.

Lounging on the couch, Abdullah and Monifah, Monifah peered into the paper bag that contained the blood money.

"Wow. That's a lot of cash. What's in the duffel bag?" she said, fixing her eyes on the huge duffel bag that rested on the floor, swiftly glancing back at the paper bag and viewing the thousands of dollars.

"Weed dat I gotta off," Abdullah answered.

*****

The following day, early in the morning, a male teenager made headway to Shyba's front door. The teen knocked on the door. After seven taps no one responded. And with that, he knocked hard and harder, and still nobody answered.

"This is shady. Why ain't they coming to the door? I know he's here 'cuz his Jag is right here," the teen uttered to himself, while he glanced at Shyba's Jaguar that was parked in front of the house.

Animatedly, the teen shouted, "Shyba!" as he checked to see if the door was unlocked. And sure enough, the front door was unlocked. Still yelling, the teen made his way into the residence. He stepped through the home as if he was on pins and needles, occasionally calling out Shyba's name. Shyba's silence made the teen assume that something was terribly wrong. Advancing from the front room to the kitchen, again calling out for Shyba, but still no progress.

Now entering the rear room, the teen winced upon viewing the bone-chilling scene, Shyba's hollow figure exhibiting a hole in his head, alongside with Coco who was in an identical position. The married couple's blood painted the walls and floors. Shell-shocked, the teen screamed in horror, dropping to his knees.

"Okay, what do we have here?" the black detective inquired, encountering a white-uniformed policeman who stood in the front room of Shyba's house that was swimming with law enforcement.

"We got two bodies in the rear of the house, a male and female with single gunshot wounds to their heads," the white-uniformed police officer related, while he led the black detective to the back of the house.

In a matter of minutes, the black detective peered at the lifeless bodies of Shyba and Coco that were side by side, sitting on the bloodied floor, leaning against the blood-spattered wall, and looking on with the emptiness in the windows of their eyes.

"The vic's brother called in, he found them," the white-uniformed lawman said dryly, as he glanced at the black detective.

"The killer clearly executed them. This was robbery, see how the safe was left open with nothing in it? The question is, was this a botched score that led to murder? Or was it a calculated robbery murder? See the .45 shells?" the Hispanic detective mused, as he pointed to the two spent shell casings that littered the floor.

"I'm willing to bet that this was a calculated robbery murder. I'll put my money on it. Shaman Wilson, aka Shyba, was not the type of guy you rob and think, 'hey, everything is gonna be fine and dandy.' He was no little fish in the streets. He was a major player in the drug trade, who always got away with murder. But maybe not. When the perps or perp stepped into this house, their mindset was murder. They knew they couldn't leave Shyba alive because he would try to seek them out to kill them. This young lady was killed because she was at the wrong place at the wrong time. She was a witness, cut and dry," the black detective expounded.

"It's a shame that this young lady had to die," the Hispanic detective said, shaking his head. "There were some prints lifted from the safe, hopefully they'll reveal who did this."

Chapter 2

Hours later, at the Wilmington Police Station, the black Detective and the Hispanic Detective eagerly stepped into a tiny room where the teen who discovered the soulless bodies of Shyba and Coco sat quietly. The two detectives smoothly settled into seats across from the teen where a table sat in between them.

"My name is Pitt, I'm a detective," the man with the dark-chocolate complexion said.

"And my name is Ortiz," the other detective followed.

"What's your name, son?" Detective Pitt asked.

"Webster Wilson," he replied.

"Okay, Webster, Shaman is your older brother, right?" Detective Pitt inquired.

"Yes," Webster said.

"What happened when you went to your brother's house?" Detective Ortiz pried.

Webster paused as he gathered himself together. "I knocked on the door and nobody answered, but I knew Shyba was there 'cuz his car was parked out front. You know what I'm saying? The door was open, so I went in. I called out Shyba's name, but nobody answered. I went to the back room, and dat's where I saw my brother Shyba and Coco dead!"

"I know this hurts, but we got to solve this as soon as possible. We got a killer or killers out there. We need to get them off the streets before they kill again," Detective Ortiz said soberly while peering into Webster's eyes.

"Was your brother having problems with anybody you know?" Detective Pitt queried.

"No," Webster retorted.

"Who would want to hurt or rob your brother?" Detective Ortiz inquired.

"I don't know," Webster replied with a puzzled facial expression. "Whoever killed Shyba, robbed him as well."

"This is really important. Was Shyba and his wife having any problems?" Detective Pitt interrogated.

"No, not dat I know of. They was cool in love, you know?" Webster answered as he got a little emotional.

*****

"Wilmington Police are investigating a double murder. Late last night around midnight a husband and wife were gunned down inside their home. The man's name, Shaman. And Carolyn Wilson! The Wilmington Police said it was a robbery execution-style shooting."

"This was a robbery homicide. The male victim was a local drug dealer, a major figure in the streets of Wilmington. Right now we're going over our leads."

"Damn they offed Shyba! I can't believe he's gone," Webster said with soreness, viewing the idiot box that displayed a homicide detective at a press conference standing in front of a podium.

"I know it don't seem real dat we ain't never gonna see Shyba come walking through the door, pulling up, banging his system! Damn," Lionel said, gravely shaking his head.

Webster's beeper blared off; he made his way to the telephone and proceeded to drum the numbers that were visible on the screen of his pager.

"Hello?"

"Somebody just page Web?" he inquired.

"Yo Dog! I just seen dat shit about your brother on the news," Abdullah exclaimed, sitting in the living room with Monifah.

"It's on, Ab. When we find out who murdered Shyba and Coco, we gonna handle dat," Webster retorted.

"What the fuck happen? On the news they said it was a robbery. Who do you think did dat shit?" Abdullah said, pretending to be in the dark.

"Man, I don't even know. Meet me at the park on 2-4 at eight eleven," Webster replied.

"All right, it's on!" Abdullah fired back.

Click! They hung up.

"What do you mean it's on? you better not be getting into no mess," Monifah said suspiciously, with her hands on her hips.

"Listen, Mo, they killed my peoples last night. It's on!"

"Retaliation is a must," Abdullah rationalized with evilness in his eyes.

"Please, Abdullah, don't do this. I don't want nothing to happen to you," Monifah said softly, with concern written all over her face.

Abdullah smiled nonchalantly, grabbing Monifah's hand, and examining the windows of her eyes.

"I love you, Mo, remember dat. Always will. You hear what I'm saying? It's gonna be all right," Abdullah said calmly as he kissed Monifah's forehead then her lips.

Monifah sighed. "Please be safe, okay?"

*****

Later on at 8:11 p.m. on the dot, Abdullah arrived at the park that sat on Tatnell Street where the streetlights glistened. Abdullah toed up the park steps, entering the park to find a handful of hooded figures dressed in black lurking in the shadows in the trench in the tail of the playground. Abdullah made his way to the rear of the park, coming face-to-face with the cloaked individuals, who flaunted monstrous frowns, as if they were ready to murder something at any given minute.

"What's the deal, Ab? You strapped?" Webster said with glassy eyes.

Abdullah simply drew a blue-steel 9mm from his waistband, cocking the lethal weapon, throwing a bullet into the chamber.

"They said it was somebody dat knew Shyba. They robbed him and everything," Webster blurted.

"We'll find them motherfuckers. Wilmington is only but so big. We'll get them niggaz," Abdullah said sternly.

Webster flashed a weak smile. "Ab, remember how we use to cut school? Remember dat time Shyba caught us? You was trickin' with dat crackhead bitch. You pulled all the strings. You made sure the basehead babe came by the crib…"

Abdullah cut Webster off before he could finish telling his story. "Yo! Web, keep it real. You fucked dat crackhead bitch raw. Nigga, I just got my dick sucked from the whore. Keep it real," Abdullah retorted as he erupted into laughter as did Webster and his crew, all except a chiseled-faced individual who towered over the hoodlums, standing at six-five.

"Fuck this shit! It's on, it's time to get them niggaz!" Carl said, the teen with the chiseled face.

"I heard it was them niggaz down the projects. The word is dat it was LB and Pete Rock. Motherfuckers was saying that on 22nd," Abdullah said deceitfully as he held a poker face.

"Let's go down the PJs. Whoever we see out there, we bust on them," Webster said vexedly, extracting from his pocket a .32 revolver, aiming the six-shooter at an invisible target.

"No, we can't do it like dat. We can't jump the gun," Lionel said firmly.

"This cat is scared. I'm ready to go down there right now. Fuck dat!" Carl barked.

"Listen, when we do shit, we gotta think. This shit is like a fucking chess game. One wrong move could get us life or send one of us to an early grave. They killed Shyba and Coco. These niggaz ain't playing, they're playing for keeps," Lionel exclaimed as he glanced at Abdullah and Webster and his crew one by one.

A tense silence invaded the air among the young hooligans while they pondered on Lionel's view.

Abdullah stared on callously, looking up at the pale moonlight through the darkish sky. *If they only knew I offed Shyba and Coco! If they only knew, these dumb-ass niggaz.* Abdullah thought to himself as he smiled inconspicuously.

"You know what, it might be a rumor about them project niggaz. We don't know if that shit is true, you know?" Webster proclaimed.

"We need the facts, Dog," Lionel replied.

"So we gonna chill until we know what went down with Shyba and Coco," Webster assented.

Chapter 3

A week later a viewing service was held for Shyba and Coco at the Congo's Funeral home on Twenty-Fourth and Market Street.

Meanwhile a block away from the depressing funeral home down on Twenty-Third and Market Street stood Abdullah by his lonesome in the darkness of the pounding rain on the side near the rear of Milton's liquor store, scheming on a way to cop some booze.

Smoothly, a man departed the van, making his way to Abdullah. "You doing something, young fellow?" the man asked.

"Yeah, whatchu need?" Abdullah replied.

"Cooked up. Let me get ten for ninety," the man fired back.

"All right," Abdullah said, as he reached inside his coat pocket, extracting a sandwich bag that contained his rocks, handing the man street candy who in return handed him United States currency. "I need you to get me a fifth of Hennessy."

Quickly, Abdullah paid the man for the liquor. And with that, the man darted off into Milton's liquor store.

Five minutes later, the man hustled back to Abdullah, who was waiting by the steps on the side of the liquor store.

"Here you go, young fellow," the man said calmly as he handed Abdullah a brown paper bag that held the bottle of liquor. "Who's selling the weed out here?"

"Right here, family, I got dat too," Abdullah relayed.

Abdullah and the man made their transaction, and then the man strolled back to his van and peeled off.

Abdullah climbed into his '85 black beat-up Chevrolet Impala, swiftly pulling off with ease, shooting down Twenty-Third Street and ending up around the corner on Twenty-Fourth Street. He parked his vehicle and stepped out onto the street into the piercing rain to be greeted by his friend, Pretty.

"What's up, Ab?" Pretty said plainly.

"Ain't nothing, Dog. I'm getting ready to walk up Chad's. Money coming?" Abdullah replied.

"Damn right!" Pretty said animatedly.

"Where everybody at?" Abdullah said, looking around.

"When it started to rain, motherfuckers jetted," Pretty fired back.

Meanwhile a teen with a bushy beard exited a row home with a boxed-in porch that lined Twenty-Fourth Street, making his way down the steps.

"What's up, Gs?" the teen with the bushy beard greeted as he encountered Abdullah and Pretty.

"Chilling, Scotty P.," Abdullah said with a slight smile.

"What's up, Scotty P?" Pretty sung.

"Whatcha got there?" Scotty P. inquired as his eyes locked on the brown paper bag that Abdullah clutched. Abdullah took a swig. "It's Henny. Here." He handed Scotty P. the brown paper bag that contained the liquor.

Scotty P. took a long drink, and then he passed the brown paper bag back to Abdullah, who took another swig while Dusty and a couple eagerly approached the young hoodlums.

"Pretty, they want seven dimes," Dusty informed.

Swiftly, Pretty led the crack fiends down the street into the cut to pursue his drug sale while Scotty P. surveyed the area for badges, as Abdullah dispersed, strolling up the street.

Abdullah stepped to a counter where a Chinese man stood behind.

"Yo! Chad let me get two blunts," Abdullah said comfortably, sliding a one-dollar bill over the counter in the tiny Chinese restaurant.

After purchasing two cigars, Abdullah stepped out of the Asian establishment onto the soaked pavement on Twenty-Fourth and Market Street as the rain palpitated the streets.

Abdullah stopped dead in his tracks at the corner of Twenty-Fourth and Market, peering up the street, observing the Congo funeral home where a few people stood out front underneath their umbrellas.

Slowly, Abdullah made his way across the intersection of Twenty-Fourth and Market Street. Now on the other side of Twenty-Fourth and Market Street, Abdullah proceeded the uphill-shaped street. Abdullah stepped into the Congo funeral home, coming face-to-face with Webster and his crew, who loitered by the front door, donned in suits with river-flowing eyes.

"I'm glad you came, Abdullah," Webster said in sadness, smiling weakly through the tears.

"Dog, it's gonna be all right. You hear me? It's gonna be all right. I'm down for whatever. Shyba was my motherfucker. We'll get pay back soon. We'll get our day, you know?" Abdullah said deviously.

Sluggishly, Abdullah walked to the front of the packed funeral home, approaching the caskets of Shyba and Coco. Three feet away from the coffin, Abdullah let out a sigh, then he stepped to Coco's casket.

"What's up, Co? Can you hear me? Shit's crazy, ain't it? Damn, you're still smoking, you know dat?" Abdullah whispered, leaning over Coco's coffin, planting a kiss onto her forehead. Goodbye."

Abdullah eased his way to Shyba's casket. "What's up, Dog? Such a dirty game. It is what it is, dat's how it is in these streets. You thought shit was sweet? You thought you couldn't be touched. Look at you now, nigga, lying on your back looking real crazy. You slept and dat's the cousin of death," Abdullah said lowly with a tauntingly voice, looking Shyba square in the face.

Slowly, Abdullah turned on his heels away from the open caskets, breezing out of the funeral home into the night, into the rain that bounced against the pavement vigorously.

Abdullah made his way back to his hooptie. He jumped into the vehicle and pulled off with ease. As Abdullah rocketed through the streets of Wilmington, Tupac Shakur's "Pain" roared out the car speakers.

"Abdullah! Yo, Abdullah!" a teenage girl shouted from the side-walk, attempting to gain Abdullah's attention.

"Girl, who dat?"

"Dat's my man! Abdullah," Sami said proudly.

"Shiiiiiiiiiit. I can't tell he kept going. He didn't stop or noth-ing." Joan wisecracked.

Now the girl Sami was extremely attractive as was Joan. They were ghetto beauties, no doubt. Sami had a honey complexion with almond eyes along with an alluring smile with a voluptuous fig-ure. Joan on the other hand had a petite frame that occupied many curves with a charming and gripping smile accompanied with a night complexion.

"Here he come now. I told you he's my man!" Sami energeti-cally said, whipping her neck.

The '85 black beat-up Chevrolet Impala crept up, pulling along-side Sami and Joan. The pair rushed to the vehicle as the window to the passenger side, slid down, displaying a figure draped in a Ronald Reagan mask clutching a firearm menacingly.

"Get in the fucking car!" the masked figure ordered, waving a 9 millimeter in the faces of Sami and Joan.

Promptly, complying with the masked figures demand, the bulged-eyed young girls climbed into the raggedy automobile as if they were zombies, settling into the back seat. Laughing uncontrolla-bly, Abdullah peeled off the Ronald Reagan mask.

"What the fuck, Abdullah? Why is you playing? You gonna scare us like dat," Sami ranted.

"This is Abdullah. You crazy for real," Joan said bluntly, frown-ing, rolling her eyes.

"Who the hell is you?" Abdullah fired back.

"I am Joan, baby. The one and only," she said conceitedly.

"Where the trees at? Smoke something," Sami said animatedly, while she jumped into the front seat.

"Listen, I got dat bomb shit. Here, roll it up," Abdullah said calmly, handing Sami a dime bag of marijuana and a Philly blunt cigar.

"Mr. crazy man, do you got a boy for me?" Joan inquired from the back seat.

"Mr. crazy man," Abdullah retorted, pulling off as he laughed. "Yeah, I got you," he added, putting his laughter in check. "What was y'all doing in the rain? What y'all trying to get money?"

"Trying to get money? We ain't trying. We getting money. We hustling, we got coke," Sami replied.

"Twenty-ninth got coke money? Listen, check this out. I got weed y'all can move, y'all down," Abdullah said with a sly smile with a bit of uncertainty in his voice.

"We could do something for you?" Sami said softly.

"We'll work something out. Pretty soon I'll have coke too. Quarters? Halfs? Ounces?" Abdullah said hurriedly.

In a matter of minutes, Sami artfully cracked open the Philly blunt cigar, spilling out its gut from the passenger window into the streets while Abdullah wheeled the Impala. Sami placed the marijuana into the hollow Philly blunt cigar, licking the roll, forming the roll as Snoop Dogg and Dog pound's, "Dog Pound for Life" blared out of the car radio speakers.

In a matter of seconds, the Philly blunt cigar was perfectly rolled. After brushing the perfectly rolled blunt cigar with the light of the lighter and putting on the finishing touches, Sami lit the blunt inhaling deeply.

As Abdullah pulled on the blunt, he shuttled up Twenty-Fourth Street, near the Chinese restaurant. Abdullah found a parking spot, smoothly pulling into the empty spot.

Out of nowhere emerged Dusty through the mist of the rainstorm, racing up to the vehicle that Abdullah occupied.

Animatedly, Dusty made hand gestures for Abdullah to roll down the driver side window, while Abdullah nonchalantly puffed on the blunt. Abdullah passed the blunt to Sami and climbed out of the '85 black beat-up Chevrolet Impala.

"What's up, Dusty?" Abdullah inquired.

"You got weed?" Dusty asked hurriedly.

"Yeah," Abdullah replied.

"Come on," a hyped-up Dusty said as he led Abdullah to a Honda Prelude where a man waited patiently. Swiftly, Dusty climbed into the vehicle with Abdullah following suit.

"My peoples got dat good shit. Bust head, I'm telling you. It's good shit, man," Dusty said persuasively from the passenger seat of the Honda Prelude.

"What can I get for two hundred?" the driver of the Honda Prelude asked, peering at Abdullah through the rearview mirror.

"I'll give you twenty-three," Abdullah replied.

"That's cool," the marijuana buyer said agreeably.

Quickly, Abdullah made the drug sale and then him and Dusty departed from the Honda Prelude.

"Can I get a little something, something?" Dusty asked.

"Why we always gotta go through this?" Abdullah said with irritation in his voice.

"Dat's what's wrong with you young boys. Y'all don't ever want to play fair," Dusty retorted.

"Dusty, stop fucking playing with me, all right?" Abdullah fired back. Where Pretty and them at?" he added.

"They in Scotty P's. Look, here they come now," Dusty said as he pointed at Pretty and Scotty P, while they toed down Scotty Ps row house steps.

A 88 Buick Reatta darted up Twenty-Fourth Street stopping in front of Scotty P's row house. Without any hesitation Scotty P. made his way to the vehicle and jumped in.

"All right Pretty, Ab", Scotty P. said from the passenger seat before the 88 Buick Reatta pulled off.

"Where he going?" Abdullah pried.

"Out Newark. Dat was his girl," Pretty relayed.

"I got somebody for you in the car. Come on, Abdullah said as he led his friend to his '85 black beat-up Chevrolet Impala.

"Ab, I hope she ain't no dog-looking bitch. Nigga, you know how you get down. You don't give a fuck, you don't discriminate at all, you'll fuck anything," Pretty teased as he laughed uncontrollably.

"Pussy don't got no face," Abdullah rationalized.

Abdullah and Pretty made their way toward Abdullah's hooptie, stopping short of his vehicle where Sami and Joan sat restfully.

"Go head, kick it to her. "She in the back seat," Abdullah provoked.

With the rain zipping from the heavens, sluggishly, Pretty strolled up to the Impala while Abdullah looked on intently.

"What's up, gorgeous girl? What's your name?" Pretty said with a smile, leaning into the slightly cracked back seat window, peering into Joan's eyes.

"What's yours?" Joan danced around the questions, not removing her eyes from Pretty's.

"Pretty," he said confidently.

"Pretty," Joan repeated, chuckling.

"Yeah, Pretty," he replied.

"I'm Joan," she said, flashing a smile.

"Ayo, Joan, you got a man?" Pretty queried.

"Nope," Joan promptly answered, shaking her head.

"Let's change dat then. Let's make something happen between us. Let me be your man," Pretty said openly.

"All right, you can be my man. Are you chilling with us tonight?" Joan said, dewy eyed.

"Yeah, I'm with y'all tonight," Pretty retorted.

"Who got the chronic?" a man asked as he approached Abdullah.

"Right here, fam. Whatchu need?" Abdullah replied, eagerly stepping to the man who sought to purchase street candy.

"Three dimes," the man confirmed.

Quickly and artfully, Abdullah drew a sandwich bag that was stuffed with marijuana. In a matter of seconds, the drug transaction was over. Subsequently, suddenly a flock of mary jane smokers rushed Abdullah.

"Abdullah, yo let me get ten."

"Let me get a quarter."

"Abdullah, you got two ounces?"

"Ab, you working with a q p?"

Abdullah was raking up dead presidents from the Shyba caper, sale after sale after sale after sale.

Dusty strolled up to Pretty. "Let me get seventeen dimes. I ain't fucking with your boy," he said with a hint of anger, briefly glancing at Abdullah.

Cool, calm, and collected, Pretty pulled out a medicine bottle, sprinkling dime rocks from the medicine bottle into his hand for display for Dusty.

"Come on, Pretty, give me the biggest ones you got. Treat me right now. It's me," Dusty sang, peering at the stones that rested on Pretty's palm.

Carefully, Dusty selected the hugest boulders, one by one, as if he were a kid in a toy store. After gathering his street candy, paying Pretty, Dusty bopped off joyfully into the rainfall.

As Abdullah and Pretty devoured riches from the weed and crack sales in the frisky rain, Sami and Joan intently observed in astonishment while they sat in the '85 black beat-up Chevrolet Impala.

"These niggaz are ballers. Pretty is sharp girl, and Abdullah is a little cutie pie," Joan exclaimed from the back seat.

"Watch your mouth, bitch. Don't be looking at him like dat. Dat's my man," Sami snapped playfully, throwing her neck side to side.

"One Time! One Time! One Time!" Dusty yelled at the top of his lungs, as he stood in the middle of the block in front of row homes, warning Abdullah and Pretty that lawmen were coming.

Slowly, a police cruiser moved up Twenty-Fourth Street.

"Yo! Let's bounce," Abdullah said, lively, while the badges drew closer.

Swiftly, Abdullah and Pretty climbed into the Impala. Abdullah peeled off at "Hoochies Need Love Too," from the *Above the Rim* soundtrack, which swam through the vehicle.

"Yo spark the billy," Abdullah said, handing Sami a perfectly rolled blunt as he stalked the rearview mirror for the authorities.

Moments later, in Newcastle, Delaware, Abdullah, Pretty, along with Sami and Joan, pulled up into a motel.

Simultaneously, Abdullah and Pretty departed the Impala to be greeted by a well-dressed man who exhibited a tar complexion loitering in front of the motel office where people checked in and out of the establishment.

"Cool guys, y'all doing something? Y'all working?" the well-dressed man solicited.

"Whatchu trying to get?" Pretty questioned.

"Cooked up, not that slab shit," the well-dressed man replied.

Sneaking to be out of view from the Indians who occupied the office and owned the motel, Abdullah, Pretty, and the well-dressed man slide to the side of the office to engage in their drug deal. Quickly, Pretty exchanged street candy for United States currency with the well-dressed man.

"My man, we need you to get us a double. What's going on? You got us?" Abdullah said plainly.

The well-dressed man smiled. "Give me the change, young-blood. I got y'all," he said.

Minutes later, the well-dressed man reverted back to the side of the motel where Abdullah and Pretty waited.

"Here's y'all keys, they didn't have any more doubles, but I got two rooms dat are connected," the well-dressed man said while he handed Abdullah and Pretty their keys to their rooms.

Meanwhile, the rainfall had ceased as Webster and Lionel prowled the dark streets of Wilmington in a '92 white Acura Legend. Webster bent a corner slowly, proceeding up Twenty-Second and Carter, encountering the block where a crowd of street players gathered around a crap game.

"Weed?" a young hustler who stood in a crowd shouted as he made hand gestures as if he was pulling on a joint.

Webster stopped in the street. "Yeah let me get two, Munch," he said, sitting behind the wheel.

Lionel jumped out of the Acura and made his way to Munch.

Swiftly, Munch handed Lionel two enormous dimes. In return Lionel passed him dead presidents.

"Alright, Dog," Lionel said, peering down at the bags of skunk his hand cupped.

Sitting at a table in the motel room in front of a window that was covered by curtains, Abdullah scanned the room, peering at Sami, who sat across the table, then glancing at pretty and Joan who lounged on the bed, as he gracefully lit the blunt that drooped from his mouth.

Simultaneously, the smoke and the aroma of the marijuana invaded the room while Abdullah inhaled and exhaled. After taking his puffs from the blunt, slightly coughing, Abdullah handed Sami the doobie who unhesitatingly inhaled.

A few pulls later Sami passed the joint to Joan. As Joan dragged on the blunt, Pretty looked on, watching her get lifted.

"You want some of this?" Abdullah asked, looking at Pretty, holding up a fifth of Hennessy.

"You know I don't drink or smoke," Pretty fired back.

"What? You don't smoke?" Joan exclaimed with disbelief in her voice.

"Nah," Pretty replied.

Joan handed Abdullah the doobie.

"Are you sure you don't want no Hennessy?" Abdullah teased, as he sipped from the bottle of liquor, inhaling the blunt.

"I'm just fucking with you," Abdullah proclaimed as he smiled.

"Come on, Abdullah. I want you to fuck the shit out of me," Sami said seductively, looking deep into his eyes, rising out of her seat.

Sami grabbed Abdullah by the hand and smoothly ushered him into the next room.

Once inside their room, Sami hit the light switch, transforming the room into complete darkness. On her knees with Abdullah standing up, Sami attempted to undo his pants.

"Hold up, Sami. Let me get my heat," Abdullah said, removing his firearm from his pants, placing the lethal weapon onto the nearby table.

Abdullah sat on the edge of the bed while Sami smoothly positioned herself in between his legs with her knees flat on the floor. Sami didn't utter a single word, swooping down to unfasten Abdullah's pants. In seconds, Sami had Abdullah's trousers off. Immediately, she rubbed her fingers against his manhood. Then she slowly inserted his Johnson into her watery mouth. She sucked him off as if she was a blood-sucking leech, while her head violently bobbed up and down.

Moments later, Abdullah was on top of Sami, embedded in between her legs, penetrating her love tunnel. Viciously, she scratched his back, while he mercilessly pounded her kitty-kat. Abdullah flipped Sami over on her stomach with her rump erected in the air, drilling his manhood into her from the back, doggy style, until he exploded, unleashing his seeds inside her.

"Yo! Ab, it's checkout time! Let's go, nigga! It's checkout time! We gotta go!" Pretty exclaimed as he knocked on Abdullah's room door.

"I've been trying to get your ass up. You told me to leave you the fuck alone and then you started pointing dat damn gun. Do you always sleep with dat thing?" Sami said sardonically, while she held her hands on her hips, whipping her neck side to side.

"Damn right, all the time," Abdullah fired back as he jumped up from the bed, proceeding to leave the motel.

Just as Abdullah glided out of the motel with Pretty occupying the passenger seat along with Sami and Joan sitting in the back seat, emerged the well-dressed man from out of the woodwork of the establishment, darting toward the rear of the '85 black beat-up Chevrolet Impala. Peering into the rearview mirror, Abdullah noticed that the well-dressed man was chasing his vehicle.

"Cool guys, y'all still working?" the well-dressed man hollered.

Abdullah stopped the Impala. "Get in," he invited.

And with that, the well-dressed man eased into the back seat, jamming Joan into the middle.

"Yo, dat was some blazing shit. Let me get twelve," the well-dressed man exclaimed with wide eyes.

"Pretty, I got six rocks left. I give him six. You give him six," Abdullah orchestrated.

Quickly, Abdullah and Pretty made their transaction, street candy for dead presidents.

*****

"Bye, Ab. Call me, baby," Sami said elatedly, while she departed from the '85 black beat-up Chevrolet Impala.

"See you, Pretty," Joan said merrily, on the trail of her friend Sami exiting the vehicle.

Abdullah and Pretty pulled off from the corner of Thirty-Third Street as Sami and Joan watched them closely missile down the block until they vanished from their sight.

"Did you hit dat?" Abdullah pried.

"Did I hit dat? You damn right I hit dat. See, Ab, I always tell them bitches what they want to hear. And a lot of times you gotta tell them what they want to hear just to get the pussy. You know what I'm saying?" Pretty retorted, smiling ear to ear.

"Nigga, you probably ate the pussy and ass. How she gonna resist a pussy licking and ass licking? She ain't gonna say no to dat, Nigga, you probably still got shit on your tongue," Abdullah wisecracked.

"Dog, it was crazy money coming last night. I creamed them," Pretty fired back, changing the subject.

Chapter 4

Posted up in front of the Chinese eatery on Twenty-Fourth and Market Street, Abdullah and Pretty meticulously observed the traffic that smoothly glided up and down the strip for any badges that mingled in the stream of vehicles. The streetlight switched red while a '91 Maroon Honda Accord LX sluggishly approached, coming to a complete stop.

"Ebony! Ebony! Ebony!" Abdullah yelled from the sidewalk, standing near the corner of Twenty-Fourth and Market Street.

H-Town's rockin, knockin tha boots blared in Ebony's Honda as she joyfully sang along. Ebony just happened to look to her right, unexpectedly discovering Abdullah standing on the corner. Immediately, Ebony read Abdullah's lips, realizing that he was calling her.

Bitterly, Ebony rolled her eyes, turning her head in disgust, planting her eyes back onto the traffic light. As the traffic light transformed to green, Ebony floored the gas, zooming through the intersection while Abdullah eagerly continued to try to gain her attention.

Coming to terms that Ebony ignored him, Abdullah screamed at the top of his lungs, "Fuck you, bitch!" as she cruised down the strip.

Watching the maroon Honda leave his sight, Abdullah exhaled as he hung his head, falling into deep thought, reminiscing.

*****

It was the summer of '91, the summer that Will Smith's "Summertime" became a household song, the anthem of all summers to proceed.

*****

Claymont, Delaware

In the midst of the suburbs, in a jam-packed glitzy carnival, Abdullah, Coby, Say Q, and Jax stood at a food stand waiting for their grub. The vendor handed Abdullah a stick of cotton candy and a soda. From behind Abdullah a finger manifested, tapping his shoulder lightly, startling him and causing him to drop his cotton candy and soda.

Immediately, Abdullah spun around to find a teenage girl with intense beauty standing at five feet tall, occupying a bronze complexion, accompanied with chinky eyes. Her frame was flawless, shaped like an hourglass displaying a round and plump rump shaker with bulging firm titties. She was half black and half Indonesian with hair pouring down the middle of her back.

"I am so sorry," she said sincerely.

"Don't worry about it. It ain't 'bout nuffin. What's your name?" Abdullah replied as the vendor handed Coby, Say Q, and Jax their food.

"Trish," she said warmly, smiling brightly.

"I'm Abdullah," he said quickly.

"Hi, Abdullah," Trish said gently, still smiling.

"Where you from?" Abdullah pried.

"West Chester, Pennsylvania. I moved to Delaware last month. I live behind Philadelphia Pike, right behind the shopping center and bowling alley," Trish informed.

"Can I come see you?" Abdullah asked.

"No, I can't let you do that. My friend likes you. See her over there?" Trish retorted as she pointed to a teenage girl who stood in front of a ferris wheel by her lonesome, while an array of people from all walks of life strolled by her. "Her name is Ebony," she added.

Ebony flaunted a dark bluish complexion. She sported spectacles, and underneath her frames were a set of pretty brown eyes with a lovely face holding shoulder-length hair. Her figure was unblemished, much thicker than Trish's exhibiting monstrous curves. She hovered at five-eight.

With happiness in her stroll, Trish led Abdullah to Ebony.

"Ebony, this is Abdullah, and Abdullah, this is Ebony," Trish introduced as she stepped back, giving the pair room to get acquainted.

"What's going on, Ebony?" Abdullah said smoothly.

"You and me. Here's my number. Call me," Ebony said openly, cutting to the chase, promptly handing Abdullah a piece of paper that contained her digits.

Peering at the tiny piece of paper, Abdullah grinned devilishly.

"When you want me to call you?" he said.

"Whenever you have time. Which should be tonight," Ebony fired back, before she strutted away with Trish seductively throwing her hips side to side.

Meanwhile, Coby, Say Q, and Jax encountered Abdullah. "Put me down, Ab, put me down," Jax exclaimed.

"Put you down? What you talking about?" Abdullah said with frowning eyebrows.

"Come on, don't play dumb. Come on. The smokin' babes you was just kicking it with," Jax retorted.

"You don't miss nothing, do you?" Abdullah said sarcastically.

"You got dat right. I don't miss nothing. And I'm damn sure not gonna miss nothing right in my mug. You dropping your food embarrassing yourself in front of the china doll," Jax wisecracked. "Nah, seriously though, hook me up with the china doll. And don't try to say dat's you, 'cuz I seen the babe with the glasses pass off her number to you."

"Man, I tried to hook you up. But she wasn't wit it. She just kept bragging 'bout her boyfriend, acting like he's the best thing since sliced bread," Abdullah said deceitfully, flaunting a poker face.

Weeks later, in Wilmington, Delaware, Abdullah stood at a telephone booth conversing with Ebony underneath the blazing sun.

"What's the deal for the weekend? I'm trying to chill with you," Abdullah said solemnly.

"Me and Trish are going skating. My mother and father are spending the entire weekend down in DC. So I am gonna have the house all to myself. Trish will be keeping me company. I want you to come over too. In fact, I need you to come over. I have a present for you. Your friend will be over to keep Trish busy," Ebony babbled, sitting in her cozy bedroom.

"Who you talking about? Who's my friend?" Abdullah queried, perplexed.

Ebony giggled. "Jax silly."

"What?" Jax goes with Trish?" Abdullah said boisterously as if he couldn't believe his ears.

"Yes. You didn't know that?" Ebony replied.

"Nah, I didn't know dat," Abdullah said dryly, before pausing for several seconds. "Dat's what's up. I'm glad Jax and Trish go together," he added while he held a facial expression that showed jealousy and envy.

"Jax is supposed to take Trish's virginity this weekend. You know, she's still a virgin," Ebony gossiped.

*****

Elsmere, Delaware

On a hot, humid night, sitting in the back seat of an '87 rusty gray Oldsmobile, Abdullah and his crew from Twenty-Second Street slid into Elsmere's crammed skating-rink parking lot.

"Meechie, keep the tool in the car," Smooth said, sitting behind the wheel of the Oldsmobile.

"Chill, man," Meechie fired back from the passenger seat, hesitatingly placing the Beretta under his seat.

Abdullah climbed out of the back seat of the '87 rusty gray Oldsmobile with Coby and Munch in toe. In seconds, simultaneously, Smooth and Meechie departed the vehicle.

As Abdullah and his crew made their way through the jumping skating rink, "I Wanna Sex You Up" by Color Me Badd thumped.

Standing at the rental office, Abdullah and his crew grabbed their skates and proceeded to walk deeper through the electrified building. While they strolled through the crowded skating rink, somebody from the sidelines screamed out to them.

"Yo, over here posse, over here posse," Badguy hollered from the snack bar accompanied by the other members of the Twenty-Second Street Gang: Richie Rich, Ant, Gill, Bubba Shan, O'Boy, Peewee,

OG, Doo doo, Big Carl, Toughy Steve Reese, House, Harry, Cooter, Chatt, Boyd, Munch, B-Love, Pookie, and RB.

"What's up, Badguy? What's up, posse?" Smooth exclaimed with a smile, greeting his crew one by one with handshakes.

As the hoodlums clutched each other's mitts, Abdullah saw something in his peripheral. Quickly, Abdullah turned to look, and there she was, in the flesh, Trish, sitting with Jax.

In that instant, jealousy and envy seeped into Abdullah's being as he watched Trish and Jax enjoying themselves, feeding one another pizza. Abdullah sighed, then he stepped toward Trish and Jax. Making his way closer to the enthusiast pair, Abdullah pictured them in between the sheets and that was a fear that gripped him.

"What's going on?" Abdullah said upon reaching the table of Trish and Jax, who sat comfortably, shoulder to shoulder.

"It's my boy, Abdullah, what's happening black? What's going on?" Jax said, vivaciously, smiling broadly.

"Chilling. I didn't know y'all went together till my girl Ebony put me down. As a matter of fact, where she at?" Abdullah replied.

"She went to the bathroom," Trish related.

Moments later, Ebony emerged from the restroom, making her way back to the table where she left Trish and Jax. As Ebony came into clear view of her table, she observed Abdullah sitting with Trish and Jax. Instantly, a smile lit up Ebony's face.

"Hey, Ab," Ebony sang, peering deep into Abdullah's eyes, then kissing his lips, as she flopped into the seat right next to him.

"Ebony. You smelling good and looking good. Show you right. It's on tonight," Abdullah chimed.

"Thank you," Ebony replied as she smiled ear to ear.

Slyly, Abdullah locked eyes with Trish for a minute before she broke the lock by looking away.

Vigorously, Abdullah sought to reconnect the gaze with Trish, who refused to let their eyes meet. Trish poured all her attention on Jax, causing Abdullah to stare into thin air intensely.

"What's wrong?" Why are you looking like you're down? Are you okay?" Ebony whispered into Abdullah's ear with concern in her voice, roping her arm around him to comfort him.

"I'm cool. I was just thinking about something. It ain't like dat," Abdullah responded with a flimsy smile.

Claymont, Delaware

Later on that night, in a middle-class town house complex in the comfort of Ebony's living room sat Abdullah on a love seat with Ebony, discreetly eyeing Trish, who idled across the room on a couch accompanied by Jax.

Abruptly, Jax and Trish exploded in a rash of passionate kisses, leading Abdullah's eyes to bug from the sight.

Swiftly, Abdullah extracted his pager from his pocket. Keenly turning it off then switching it back on, making the loot clocker go off as if someone was paging him.

"Yo let me see the horn," Abdullah said excitedly.

"Come on it's in the kitchen," Ebony quickly replied, as she ushered Abdullah to the kitchen.

Abdullah and Ebony stepped into the kitchen. Immediately, Abdullah snatched the telephone from it's cradle, promptly drumming the numbers.

"What? They jumped on Coby and CS! Who? Where y'all at?"

"All right, we'll be there. I'm out," Abdullah ranted, putting on an elaborate performance as if he were talking to somebody, but in reality really wasn't.

"What happened? Ab, what's wrong?" Ebony pried, with concern in her face and voice.

"Motherfuckers hopped on my bol's, go get Jax it's getting ready to be on," Abdullah barked.

*****

Meanwhile, in the living room, Trish and Jax were getting hot, heavy, and steamy.

"I am ready, Jax. I am ready. Let's do it, let's go upstairs." Trish panted as she grabbed Jax by the arm.

Jax simply gazed at Trish, not uttering a single word. It was all in the windows of his eyes that he longed for her, all in the windows of his eyes that he wanted her badly. Jax scooped Trish from off the couch, holding her in his arms. He shot straight up the steps, then into the bedroom.

"Do you love me?" Trish asked naively, as she commenced to disrobe.

"Without a doubt, I do," Jax smoothly and quickly replied. "Here, put this in," he added, while he handed Trish a tape to put into the radio.

Trish inserted the tape into the tape deck, turning the power on. "Love you down" by Ready for the World invaded the room as Trish laid on the bed naked.

Now in his birthday suit, Jax positioned himself on top of Trish, sliding his tongue into her ear and then into her mouth. Gradually, Jax made his way down to Trish's neck, slurping on her flesh as if he were a blood-sucking vampire while she hummed out moans of gratification. Jax licked his way to Trish's melons, placing them into his mouth one by one.

"You like dat, baby? I'm gonna make you love me forever," Jax muffled violently, licking and sucking Trish's breasts.

"Don't stop, Jax. It feels so good," Trish whispered.

Boom! Boom! Boom! Boom! Boom! Boom! Boom!

"Jax! Jax! Jax! Hey, Jax! Abdullah wants you. Y'all boys just got a beatdown. Coby and CS!" Ebony exclaimed.

*****

Meanwhile, in the kitchen, Abdullah paced nervously back and forth. As Abdullah waited for Jax, he envisioned Jax having Trish pinned up with her legs in the air, mercilessly pounding her love box.

"Hold up, here I come," Jax hollered as he leaped off Trish, hastily throwing his clothes back on.

"Wait a minute, where are you going?" Trish snapped.

"Chill, you heard your girl. My boys got into some shit I'll be back," Jax replied.

Energetically, Jax walked into the kitchen. "What's up, duke?" Jax sang, displaying a smile.

Did this nigga get the pussy or something? Why he smiling like dat? Abdullah thought to himself.

"Them Chester bols fucked Coby and CS up. They want us to meet them at the Claymont High's racetrack," Abdullah said, looking at Jax square in the eyes.

Abdullah and Jax stepped onto Claymont High's racetrack, which sat directly behind Ebony's town house.

"Coby and CS and them should be here any minute," Abdullah said, breaking the silence that lingered in the night air, looking away from Jax. "We been here ten minutes," he added.

"Where did Coby and CS get jumped at?" Jax pried.

"Out Stoneybrook at Sha Juan's crib. The whole crew was at the spot, Carol, Nichelle, La, Robin, Kisha. Coby and C.S got the dog-shit beat out of them. I think them chicks set them bols up," Abdullah proclaimed.

"Dat's crazy," Jax fired back with anger in his voice.

"Did you fuck her? Did you fuck Trish yet?" Abdullah abruptly asked, changing the subject.

"Not yet, I was about to hit it though. I'm gonna hit it later on, word I am. The pussy can wait, it's gonna be there. My boys need me right now!" Jax answered.

"I'll say dat's right," Abdullah retorted.

A half hour slipped by in the dark, muted racetrack where the empty bleachers were situated.

Standing outside the racetrack, footsteps away from the unoccupied bleachers, Abdullah intensely stared through the gloom at the rear of Ebony's town house as Jax strolled around the racetrack.

After lapping the course numerous times, Jax decided to quit, making his way to Abdullah, and while Abdullah continued to scope out Ebony's house Jax approached from behind.

"Ab, I'm gonna wait five minutes. If Coby and CS don't show I'm out," Jax declared, standing a foot away from Abdullah, looking at the back of his head.

Suddenly, with the speed of light, Abdullah spun around and heartlessly plunged a knife into Jax's stomach. Slowly, Jax peered down at his stomach to discover a blade lodged into it with Abdullah gripping the handle. With disbelief and horror leaping from the windows of his eyes, Jax looked up at Abdullah as if he couldn't comprehend that his longtime friend had just thrust a knife into his abdomen. Before Jax could blink, Abdullah pulled the dagger out of his stomach and viciously drove the steel back into his gut, again, again, again, again, and again.

Jax folded to his knees, then he crashed face-first to the ground. Nonchalantly, Abdullah extracted a handkerchief from his pocket, carefully wiping his fingerprints from the bloody knife. Then Abdullah tossed the deadly weapon to ground before dashing away into the night, leaving Jax to die.

Abdullah sprinted to Ebony's townhouse as if he were being pursued by Jason from the flick *Friday the 13th*.

Once Abdullah reached Ebony's front doorstep, he struck the door and shouted until somebody responded.

"Who is it?" answered a sweet little voice.

"It's Abdullah! Let me in!" he exclaimed.

And with that, the door swung open revealing Trish, who stood in a skin-tight shirt and panties while inviting Abdullah into the residence.

"What's going on? Where's Jax? And why was you banging on the door like you lost your mind?" Trish interrogated, with her hands resting on the rear of her hips.

"We got chased by them Chester cats. They was twenty deep. I told Jax to meet me back here. We ran our separate ways," Abdullah replied as he looked into Trish's eyes.

"Well, why isn't Jax here yet? Abdullah do you think they caught Jax? He isn't here?" Trish said abruptly, panic leaping from her voice.

"No, no, he'll be here. Jax can run, they won't catch him. I'm telling you, he's fast," Abdullah asserted.

"I am starting to get scared. I think something happened to Jax. I have this really bad feeling," Trish proclaimed with fear in her eyes

"Wait up for him, he'll be here," Abdullah said coolly, as he made his way up the stairs.

Abdullah strolled into the bathroom. He peered into the mirror, searching his eyes, standing there in a trancelike state for about three minutes before splashing his face with water.

Abdullah eased his way into Ebony's bedroom where she stood near her bed, singing along with Patti Labelle's "Somebody Loves You Baby." As soon as Ebony noticed Abdullah standing there, she immediately raced into his arms.

"Hey, is everything okay?" Ebony said softly, looking Abdullah square in the eyes, while her arms roped around his neck.

Abdullah sighed, as he lowered his gaze with Ebony. "We got chased by them Chester bols. They was about twenty strong. I don't know if they caught Jax... If they did, all man. I hope he got ghost on them cats."

"What about your other friends, Coby and CS? What happened to them? Are they okay?" Ebony inquired.

"Oh my God! No, no, please help! Help, somebody! Help me, somebody! Ebony! Abdullah, help!"

"Abdullah, did you hear that? Sounds like someone is hollering," Ebony said suspiciously, as she turned down the radio.

"Nah, I didn't hear nothing," Abdullah replied.

"No! No! Noooo! Help! I need help, help me, oh God!"

"That's Trish! Come on!" Ebony exclaimed with bugged eyes, realizing that something was terribly wrong.

Ebony darted out of the bedroom with Abdullah on her heels. The pair feverishly rushed through the corridor. In a matter of minutes, they reached the edge of the top of the stairs. Trish's dreadful screams grew louder and louder as Abdullah and Ebony toed down the steps. Upon placing their feet onto the floor, the twosome encountered a hideous stream of blood. The bloody trail ran from the front door to the bathroom. Abdullah and Ebony froze as they took in the grim view, scanning the room for Trish, who was nowhere in sight.

Trish's howling ceased as silence and suspense filled the air. Subsequently, Ebony broke out in tears.

"Abdullah, where is Trish? I'm scared for her," Ebony said warily, tears dropping out of her eyes profusely.

Abdullah shook his head. "Things don't look good," he said pessimistically, as he led the way to the bathroom with Ebony in tow.

It seemed like an eternity for the teenage couple with their eyes intently rolling over the red watery path as they gradually inched closer to the bathroom. Now three steps away from the bathroom, trembling uncontrollably, Ebony grabbed Abdullah's hand.

"Don't worry about a thing, I'm here," Abdullah assured.

"Abdullah, do you think Trish is okay?" Ebony asked quietly with tears and uncertainty in her eyes.

"I don't know," Abdullah replied, looking away from Ebony.

Abdullah and Ebony entered the bathroom to be greeted by a distraught Trish, who was drenched in blood, clutching Jax in her arms.

Desperately, Jax attempted to speak, but blood gushed out of his mouth instead of words.

"It's all right, baby. You're gonna be all right. You're gonna be just fine," Trish encouraged, holding Jax and trying to comfort him.

Abdullah and Ebony stopped dead in their tracks as they viewed the horror show.

This nigga can't pull through. He gots to die! Abdullah thought to himself as he kneeled down in front of Jax.

"Jax, man, I'm here. You can't give up. Help is coming, hold on," Abdullah said calmly, peering into Jax's face.

Jax's body started to fidget while he again tried to speak.

"You called 911, right?" Abdullah queried, looking directly into Trish's eyes.

"Yes, I did," Trish said sadly, focusing her eyes on her wounded boyfriend. "Jax, do not die on me. I need you, don't you dare! Please don't leave me, please, I need you."

Abruptly, Jax spoke, "Why me?" he said weakly as his body convulsed.

Stop fighting it, homie. Let go, it's over, Abdullah thought to himself, watching in amusement with a half smirk, Jax's body jolting vigorously.

Then suddenly Jax's convulsions came to a halt. He took a breath then he twitched as the Angel of Death snatched his soul.

"No! Don't go. I love you, Jax! Jax! Jax! No, you can't die on me!" Trish lamented as she frantically rocked Jax back and forth in her arms, tears racing down her face.

"He's gone, Trish. Let him go. It's gonna be all right," Abdullah said quietly, gently, and consolingly. Resting his hand on Trish's shoulder, then burying her into his arms.

Swiftly, Trish broke out of Adbullah's embrace. "It's all your fault. If you didn't take Jax to Claymont High racetracks, this would have never happen. I hate you!" she roared, shoving Abdullah with all her might.

"It ain't my fault Jax got killed. It ain't my fault. Don't be putting dat shit on me. Dat was my fucking roadie. You better go 'head with dat shit," Abdullah countered.

"Come on, you two, it's no need to be arguing. It's nobody fault that Jax is dead. Come on. Just look at this picture."

"Trish, you blaming Ab isn't gonna bring Jax back. Don't you think Ab feels terrible? Jax was his friend," Ebony said firmly as her eyes bounced back and forth from Trish to Abdullah, Abullah to Trish, back to Abdullah.

Two weeks later, in the quarters of Ebony's bedroom on her bed, dwelled her and Abdullah engaging in foreplay, Abdullah's hands resting underneath Ebony's shirt, fondling her humongous titties. Their tongues were wrestling aggressively with her mitts inside of his pants, exploring his manhood. Then suddenly out of the blue Ebony popped the big question.

"What's the deal with you? I see the way you look at Trish. You're in love with her, aren't you? You love her, don't you?" Ebony said dryly, pulling away from Abdullah and removing her hands from his pants, peering deep into her eyes, searching for the truth.

"Yo! You is really bugging yo! You talking crazy now. I don't love dat girl!" Abdullah ranted.

"If you're not in love with her and you don't love her, then why do you look at her the way you do? Clearly it's in your eyes, Ab. I am not stupid!" Ebony fired back.

"Stop fucking playing with me, man!" Abdullah said irritatingly, hopping off the bed.

Abdullah stood directly in front of the bed gazing at Ebony. *Do you really think I'm in love with Trish? Do you know what time it is*" he thought to himself.

Ebony stared right back at Abdullah. *Are you playing with me? Do you love me? Do you even care about me? I wish I had the answers. I love you so much. Perhaps I'm jumping to conclusions about you being in love with Trish*, she thought to herself.

As the pair eyed one another intently, Phyllis Hyman's "Living in Confusion" leaped from the radio. The Phyllis Hyman's cut faded. Then Tracy Spencer's "Tender Kisses" invaded the room.

"I'm so confused, and I think I'm gonna cry tonight. What must I do, baby?" Ebony sang, grabbing Abdullah's hand, pulling him on top of her.

"Ab, what I told you on the phone last night, I really meant it. I love you," Ebony whispered into Abdullah's ear.

"For real?" Abdullah replied.

"For real! I love you. I care about you so much. You just don't know," Ebony said, while she started to kiss Abdullah's neck passionately.

Ebony sucked Abdullah's neck until it became red, then she put her lips on his lips. She sucked and kissed his bottom lip, then she sucked and kissed his top lip. Ebony eased her tongue into Abdullah's mouth. While their tongues tussled, Ebony slid her pants down, revealing her bush.

Eagerly Abdullah rubbed Ebony's kitty cat. In a matter of seconds, Abdullah inserted his finger into Ebony's love tunnel, leading her to moan in complete pleasure.

"Do you have a condom?" Ebony panted while Abdullah violently finger-popped her.

"Nah, I don't got one," Abdullah replied.

"Then we can't do it," Ebony said firmly as she rose up, pulling away from Abdullah.

"Why not?" Abdullah asked with frustration in his voice and face.

"Because, Abdullah, I don't want to get pregnant," Ebony justified.

"Hold up. I thought you love me," Abdullah fired back.

"I do," Ebony said hurriedly.

"All right. If you love me like you say you do, you gotta listen to me. You gotta trust me. I got this, you're not gonna get pregnant. I won't cum in you. I'll pull out, all right?" Abdullah manipulated.

"Promise me that you'll pull out," Ebony said softly.

"I promise. Come on!" Abdullah said avidly.

Smoothly, Ebony laid on her back, spreading her legs wide open. Promptly, Abdullah dove on top of Ebony, sliding his manhood into her love box. Abdullah pounded Ebony's love tunnel as if he were trying to demolish her insides. She howled his name in sheer pleasure while he fiercely stroked away.

Within a matter of minutes, Adbullah unloaded his seeds into Ebony's warmth, crumbling on top of her, rolling over, lying next to her.

Immediately, Ebony sprang from the bed, gazing at Abdullah in complete dismay.

"Why the hell didn't you pull out? I can't believe you just did that!" Ebony barked with regret and anger in her eyes.

"My fault, it was feeling too good. I couldn't pull out. Oh shit!" Abdullah replied, as he peered at his watch. "I gotta go. I gotta do something. I'll be back."

"What do you got to do? What's so important that you have to up and leave me all of the sudden?" Ebony interrogated.

"I can't tell you, it's business," Abdullah answered.

"Top secret? Yeah right. You better come back. Why are you smiling? I am not playing, Abdullah," Ebony retorted with a serious facial expression.

"I'm smiling 'cuz you look crazy when you try to look hard?"

"Nah, for real though, I gotta take care of something, word," Abdullah expounded.

Chapter 5

The next day

It was six in the morning when Ebony awoke. After showering and brushing her teeth, Ebony anxiously paged Abdullah. An hour flew by without Abdullah responding to Ebony's page. Vexed by Abdullah's missing in action after their little episode, Ebony paged him repeatedly.

"What the hell's going on? Why isn't he answering my pages? Where the hell are you, Ab?" Ebony muttered to herself in frustration.

And just like that, days smoothly slipped into a month and the month transcended into months without Ebony seeing or hearing a single word from Abdullah, leading her to become extremely bitter toward him.

Thirteen months later in Wilmington, Delaware, on the north side of town in a McDonald's restaurant sat Ebony and Trish gracefully eating their fish sandwiches when Abdullah by his lonesome strutted into the establishment. As Abdullah made his way to the counter, Trish noticed him.

"Look, girl! There go Abdullah," Trish exclaimed.

"Where?" Ebony asked with zeal, surveying the McDonald's restaurant.

*****

"See him right there?" Trish replied animatedly, pointing toward the counter where Abdullah stood.

"I see that no-good scum bastard. He's nobody," Ebony ranted as she looked Abdullah up and down from a far with disdain.

"Well, aren't you gonna say something to him?" Trish asked, tilting her head with a facial expression that read, "What are you waiting for? Give him a tongue-lashing."

"Should I?" Ebony said with a dumbfound look.

"Of course you should, he's been ignoring you for thirteen months and what not let's see if his punk ass has an excuse for abandoning your relationship," Trish insisted.

"I can't stand him. He thinks he's all that," Ebony proclaimed, glaring at Abdullah.

Abdullah had no idea that he was being eyeballed by Ebony and Trish while he arrogantly pulled out a huge knot of dead presidents to pay for his food.

"Punk-ass Abdullah! Why the hell you didn't never come back or call?" Ebony shouted bitterly, making a scene in the McDonald's restaurant.

"Who the fuck you think you talking to like dat, bitch?" Abdullah barked.

"I'm talking to you. You ain't nobody," Ebony fired back, as she bolted toward Abdullah, swinging wildly, eagerly trying to make her haymakers connect.

Quickly, Abdullah dodged and blocked Ebony's punches as the people in the McDonalds looked on. Abdullah smoothly grabbed a tray from the counter.

"If you don't chill, I'm gonna hit you with this," Abdullah warned, menacingly waving the tray in the air.

"So you hit girls now? Huh?" Ebony said sarcastically.

"Listen, the reason why I ain't come back 'cuz I was locked up," Abdullah justified with a solemn facial expression.

"For real? You was in the jail?" Ebony responded as a smile over took her facc.

"Damn. What did you do?" Trish pried.

"Yeah, what happened? I hope you didn't drop the soap in there," Ebony teased.

"I ain't drop no soap. Come on now! Listen, it's a long story. I'll tell y'all later. I'm just glad to be free. I'm glad to be back with you, Ebony," Abdullah proclaimed as he sighed.

Moments later, Abdullah, Ebony and Trish stepped out of McDonald's onto the pavement, into the blistering heat with Abdullah leading the way. The trio slowly strolled through the parking lot of the establishment where they came upon a '92 candy-apple red BMW 525i. Coolly, Abdullah made his way to the luxurious automobile, opening the driver's side door while Ebony's and Trish's mouths hung to the ground in amazement.

"Is y'all rolling?" Abdullah asked after he climbed into the driver's seat.

"Whose car is this?" Ebony interrogated with suspicion written all over her face.

"You all in dat? It ain't stolen. Y'all coming with me? Is y'all rolling or what?" Abdullah retorted, persuasively opening the passenger door along with the back door, slightly smiling.

Abdullah turned the key in the ignition, bringing the automobile to life. Ebony and Trish hesitated to hop into the running vehicle, but eventually they did.

With Ebony situated in the passenger seat and with Trish sitting comfortably in the back seat, Abdullah slyly adjusted the rearview mirror so he could get a clear sight of Trish. As Abdullah slickly gloated at Trish, he slid a tape into the tape deck.

Keith Sweat's "There you go telling me no again" invaded the Beamer.

"Where y'all wanna go?" Abdullah inquired.

"Just drive, and this car better not be stolen," Ebony said firmly.

Abdullah wheeled the '92 candy-apple red BMW 525i out of the McDonald's parking lot, shooting straight up Market Street toward Philadelphia Pike.

Keith Sweat's "There you go telling me no again" ended. As Abdullah's eyes locked with Trish, he rewound the Keith Sweat track.

Trish, I gotta have you, Abdullah thought to himself, replaying Keith Sweat's song, peering at Trish through the rearview mirror.

Is he trying to tell me something? Is he sending me a message through his song? Why in the world is he looking at me like that? With the goo-goo eye's, Trish thought to herself as she stared at Abdullah.

I wonder what Abdullah did to go to jail? Is he lying about being locked up? Whose car is this? You know what? I really don't care. I'm just glad he's back in my life, Ebony though to herself, gazing out of the passenger-side window.

Now in Claymont, Delaware, Abdullah pushed the beamer as if he was on top of the world, unconcernedly shooting pass the police station perpetrating the fraud as a licensed driver.

Artfully and hastily, Abdullah switched lanes playing the part of speed racer pressing his foot against the pedal increasing the speed exceeding past the twenty-five speed limit, doing seventy-five.

"Slow down, Ab. You're going too fast!" Ebony exclaimed as she grabbed the side of the door, bracing herself.

"Hold on," Abdullah said, hurriedly weaving in and act of traffic, sliding down Philadelphia Pike.

"Chill! Stop driving wild. Chill," Trish cried out from the back seat.

"What are y'all afraid of, huh?" Abdullah teased with a grin, recklessly maneuvering the BMW.

"Getting killed. You're driving like a damn maniac, and I do not want to die," Ebony fired back hysterically.

"The cops! The cops! There go the cops. Slow down! Abdullah, slow down!" Trish yelled, as she animatedly moved back and forth in the back seat, spotting two police cruisers up the road that was parked in front of a gas station.

"Chill, I got this. We all right," Abdullah said confidently, lifting his foot from the metal, slowing down.

As Abdullah drew near the gas station where the two squad cars were posted, his heart bounced uncontrollably. Abdullah looked into the rearview mirror, to be greeted by the worried eyes of Trish. They intensely locked eyes for minutes, then Trish looked away.

Abdullah's eyes jumped back and forth from the windshield to the rearview mirror while he glided by the service station. Once Abdullah passed the gas station, he intently peered into the rearview mirror, quickly noticing that the two squad cars were unoccupied.

Simultaneously and ungovernably, Ebony and Trish looked back from their seats, also realizing that there wasn't a single soul seated in the police cruisers.

"Don't look back," y'all gonna get us pulled the fuck over by doing dat shit," Abdullah said as he kept his eyes glued to the rear-view mirror, wheeling the Beemer up Philadelphia Pike.

"We got your back, Ab," Trish said softly.

"Get it together. We was just looking out for the cops. We do have your best interest at heart, you know?"

"But tell us this. If this car isn't stolen, hotshot, why are you so worried about getting pulled over? Huh?" Ebony said sardonically.

"'Cuz I don't got no license, dat's why. I ain't trying to get a ticket. The ride is legit. Check it. I just got out. I ain't trying to go through the bullshit. You know what I'm saying?" Abdullah explained, shaking his head.

Chapter 6

Moments later near the main line leading toward Chester, Pennsylvania, Abdullah accompanied by Ebony and Trish pulled into the Tri State Malls parking lot.

Abdullah parked the BMW in front of a Kmart that lined the Tri State Mall. Abdullah peered into the rearview mirror, slickly gazing at Trish. As their eyes met, Abdullah shot Trish a wink, who swiftly dismissed his advance with a frown followed by a smirk, whipping her head and looking away. Abdullah chuckled.

"What the hell are you laughing at?" Ebony questioned with raised eyebrows.

"It ain't bout nuffin. I was just thinking about something," Abdullah hurriedly answered.

"If this car is stolen, you'll really have something to think about," Ebony wisecracked.

Simultaneously, Ebony and Trish erupted in laughter, laughing at Ebony's remark.

Abdullah and the two girlfriends entered the mall, coming face-to-face with a golden-complexioned teen who sported a rounded high-top fade that displayed a patch of gray in the front.

"What's going down?" the golden-complexioned teen exclaimed.

"What's up, Reishee?" Abdullah replied.

Abdullah and Reishee shook each other's hands and embraced.

Reishee swung his arm around Abdullah, leading him away from Ebony and Trish.

"When you get out?" Reishee inquired.

"Three days ago," Abdullah responded.

"Yeah," Reishee said, flashing a smile.

"Yeah man," Abdullah said calmly.

"So you fresh out, huh?" "I see you got the hotties with you," Reishee said smoothly, fixing his eyes on Ebony and Trish. "Which one is you?"

"The taller one with the glasses. But I'm gonna get the other one, she's gonna be mine," Adbullah informed.

Reishee smiled ear to ear. "Ab, they smokin'," Reishee replied upon pausing, lusting on the young girls' striking beauty.

"I'ma see you later on. I gotta make these moves. I'm on a time limit, word," he quickly added.

"Where you gonna be later on tonight?" Abdullah inquired.

"Up Chester. Just page me, and we'll hook up. All right? I'm out," Reishee said coolly, firmly shaking Abdullah's hand before strolling out of the mall.

"Who was that?" Ebony queried with a frown.

"Girl, you better stop making you face look like dat before it stay like dat," Abdullah joked.

"Ha, ha, ha…very funny," Ebony said dryly.

"Nah, dat's my bol, Reishee. We was locked up together in the youth study center," Abdullah related.

"You guys are truly baby criminals," Trish uttered.

They all laughed at Trish's frank comment.

Juice is playing in an hour. The movie is on me. I got y'all," Abdullah proclaimed.

*****

In a dark, crammed theater sat Abdullah in between Ebony and Trish with his arm lassoed around Ebony. Several minutes into the movie, Abdullah turned to Ebony and wrapped his shoulder around her while he intently watched the flick.

"I'm going to the bathroom," Ebony announced, climbing out of her seat, heading to the lavatory.

Abdullah took a deep breath, then he faced Trish, who looked straight ahead as if she were in a deep trance.

"Listen, Trish, I've been doing a lot of thinking and I want—"

"I can't mess with you," Trish interrupted, stopping Abdullah in his tracks, avoiding eye contact. "You're Ebony's boyfriend, and I can't do that to her."

"Trish, can you just listen to what I gotta say? I love you, and I always have. From the first time I saw you. The truth is I don't love Ebony, never did, never will. I wanna be with you and only you," Abdullah said softly.

Stunned and caught off guard by Abdullah's heart-penetrating words, Trish slowly turned around to face him, peering deep into his eyes. "What about Ebony?" Trish questioned warily while she searched Abdullah's eyes.

"Don't worry about her, we'll figure something out. But we gotta be together no matter what. It's our destiny," Abdullah replied.

"I don't know, Ab. Chill, here comes Ebony," Trish said, gesturing for Abdullah to be quiet.

"Did I miss anything?" Ebony asked as she settled into her seat.

"They just robbed a store, Tupac killed the old man running the store, murdered his bol Raheem, Pac is buck wild in this joint," Abdullah informed.

"I thought Raeem was Tupac's boy," Ebony said confusingly.

"He was. Apparently that didn't matter to Tupac 'cause he's a sociopath," Trish said.

"Shush! Be quiet, y'all. Let's just watch this shit," Abdullah said, frowning.

*****

Moments later, as Abdullah watched the flick, he felt eyes piercing his face. He turned his head to the side, and there was Trish staring intensely. Trish blushed upon locking eyes with Abdullah. Simultaneously, Abdullah and Trish fixed their eyes back on to the big screen.

Abdullah's thoughts ran through his head like a wildfire devouring a forest. He pictured him and Trish at a park clutching hands, them deeply in love. He pictured Trish having his babies; he envisioned Trish as his loving wife. Then reality paralyzed Abdullah's dreams. He was back in the jam-packed theater watching *Juice*. Abdullah sighed.

Trish's mental flashed with the memories of Jax, the vision of their near encounter at the carnival. Followed by an encounter at a house party that led to a phone number swap that developed into a loving ironclad relationship, ultimately coming to a crashing halt with Jax perishing in Trish's arms.

Rest in peace, Jax. It's been over a year since you been gone. I have to move on with my life. I want to be happy now, Trish thought to herself.

Chapter 7

A man in a crowd shouted out to Omar Epps, "You got the juice!"

Swiftly, Omar Epps threw on his hood and turned on his heels. And with that, Abdullah, Ebony, and Trish stormed out of the packed theater.

"Dat jawn was alright, but they didn't have to kill the bol pac in the end, I didn't like dat part," Abdullah opinionated.

"It ended how it was supposed to end, the villain got what he deserved," Ebony asserted as they converged through the mall.

"That was a good movie, I enjoyed it." Trish inputted.

As Abdullah, Ebony and Trish cleared the first set of glass doors near the front entrance of the mall. Abdullah immediately jumped onto the pay phone.

"Who are you calling?" Ebony asked with a puzzled facial expression.

"Don't worry about it," Abdullah smart-mouthed, displaying a smile.

*****

Nightfall, Philadelphia, Pennsylvania, on 3rd and Sedgley street sat Reishee in a 86 Black Cadillac fleetwood accompanied with a roughish, but pretty creole complexioned girl who was in her late teens.

"He wants to meet me at Seventh and Allegheny," she declared from the passenger seat of the Cadillac.

"Dat's where we're gonna grab him at. Take this," Reishee replied as he handed his companion a firearm, pulling off with ease.

Reishee rocketed through the streets of Philadelphia. Moments later, he dropped off his sidekick near Seventh and Allegheny.

In a matter of minutes, Reishee's companion encountered a man who was in his midforties.

"Gwen, I didn't think you was gonna show up," the older man said with surprise lingering in his voice.

"I had to show up, Daddy, to give you some of this young ripe pussy. Daddy, you think you can handle it?" Gwen retorted seductively, flashing a smile.

"Damn right I can handle it," the older man fired back, mesmerized by Gwen's pleasing features.

"Can you handle this?" Gwen said calmly as she slyly produced a lethal weapon, discretely pressing the firearm against the man's stomach.

"Ho... Hold the hell up, what's this about?" The older man exclaimed in shock with bugged eyes.

From out of nowhere, Reishee pulled up alongside the pair, cracking the door leading to the back seat.

"Get in the car," Gwen ordered, gesturing with her head toward the rear seat of the waiting Cadillac as a few people marched up and down the City of Brotherly Love's pavement while she secretly and artfully held a pistol to his belly.

Unhesitatingly, the older man complied, falling into the back seat with Gwen sliding right next to him menacingly holding him at gunpoint.

Reishee pulled into a dark alleyway and climbed out of the Cadillac. With her firearm leveled at the older man's stomach, Gwen directed the man out of the Cadillac with the threat of being pumped with lead. Then she followed suit.

"What's going down, Strickland?" Reishee greeted, drawing a chrome .380 from his waistband, firing a round at Strickland's feet, barely missing them by inches. "Get in the fucking trunk!"

"You heard him, motherfucker! Get your old ass in there!" Gwen ranted, pressing the muzzle of her lethal weapon against Strickland's head.

Held at point blank-range in an obscure Philadelphia alley, Strickland timidly climbed into the trunk. Nonchalantly, Reishee slammed the lid of the trunk. Confining Strickland like a wild animal. Reishee and Gwen reverted back to the '86 Black Cadillac. Reishee pulled off with ease.

*****

In completed silence, Abdullah, Ebony and Trish stood around the pay phone.

"Ab, how long do you plan on waiting for this person to respond?" Ebony broke the silence with irksomeness in her voice, as she rolled her eyes, glancing at her watch.

"The person is my bol, Reishee, we ain't gonna be waiting that long," Abdullah retorted.

"If you say so," Ebony said sarcastically.

"Yo, Ebony, is it dat time of the month or something?" Abdullah countered.

Subsequently, the pay phone erupted in rings.

"I told you it wouldn't be long," Abdullah said with cockiness in his voice, snatching the telephone from the hook, flashing Ebony with a broad smile.

"Yo!" Abdullah sang into the receiver.

"What's up? Where you at?" Reishee said excitedly.

"I'm still at the mall, we just saw *Juice*. You see dat yet?" Abdullah replied.

"Nah, I wanna see it though," Reishee answered. "Yo, meet me in Chester, I got something for you."

"All right, peace," Abdullah said plainly.

"Peace, my nigga," Reishee followed.

Click! They hung up.

Abdullah placed the receiver back onto the hook and spun around to find Ebony standing in his face an inch away. Aggressively, Ebony took Abdullah's hands in hers, while he sneaked a peek at Trish, who looked straight ahead, paying the pair no mind.

"I know you're not acting funny, 'cause people are around," Ebony teased as she tightened her grip.

"A yo girl! What you trying do, break my hand or something?" Abdullah said with irritation leaping from his voice as he pulled his hand out of the mitt lock, shaking it as if it were up in flames.

"Ab, I am only playing. You know I love you," Ebony said softly and sweetly as she smiled ear to ear.

Ebony was ecstatic that Abdullah stepped back into her life. The revelation of Abdullah being incarcerated put Ebony's speculation of rejection, abandonment, and exploitation to bed. The thoughts of being played like a piano no longer lingered in her mind, but something kept nagging at her mind.

Abdullah is hiding something, but what is it? Something isn't right, why was he in jail? Ebony thought to herself as she, Trish, and Abdullah strolled from the mall toward the '92 candy-apple Red BMW 525i.

The trio climbed into the Beemer. Abdullah eased the key of the BMW into the ignition, waking the '92 candy-apple Red BMW 525i from its sleep. Smoothly, he slid Scarface into the tape deck, pulling out of the parking spot.

As Scarface's, "Born Killer" thumped from the speakers, Ebony and Trish bopped to the electrifying beat as if they were in a club while Abdullah wheeled the vehicle through the parking lot wildly. Minutes later Abdullah, along with Ebony and Trish, were on the bustling highway heading to Chester, Pennsylvania. Abdullah rocketed the BMW through traffic. Before Ebony and Trish knew it, they were taking in the sights of Chester. Abdullah hooked a turn into a gas station, smoothly pulling alongside a pay phone. Animatedly, Abdullah hopped out of the BMW, leaving the engine running, making his way to the pay phone, slamming twenty-five cents into talk machine.

"Ebony, what's Ab up to? Why does he keep jumping on all these phones?" Trish inquired while eyeing Abdullah. "I hope he's not doing anything criminal," she added.

"Girl, I don't know what he's up to," Ebony replied as she sighed.

Within minutes, the telephone booth rang out. Abdullah snatched up the telephone.

"Yo!" he sang into the receiver.

"What's up? Where you at?" Reishee said plainly.

"I'm at the gas station when you first come into Chester," Abdullah relayed.

"Meet me in front of Chester High, I'm driving a black caddy," Reishee said quickly.

Click! The friends hung up.

Abdullah climbed back into the '92 candy-apple red BMW 525i and smoothly pulled off. While Abdullah shoved the Beemer through the frigid streets of Chester with Scarface's "Dear Diary" roaring from the car speakers, he reached up underneath his seat, grabbing a TEC-9.

Immediately, Ebony's eyes grew wide from observance of Abdullah placing a lethal weapon on his lap.

Abdullah put his finger to his lips, gesturing for Ebony's silence. Then he shot her a wink, followed by a devilish grin.

Abdullah's menacing demeanor troubled Ebony to her core. She couldn't believe the person she was in love with had a deadly weapon in his possession. Now she saw the side of him she could never imagine she would. She struggled with her emotions. A part of Ebony's being told her that she could never ever deal with Abdullah after the night ended, but the other part of her being refused to let go. While her inquiry into Abdullah imprisonment intensified.

Trish sat in the back seat, completely unaware that a lethal weapon rested in Abdullah's lap. Abdullah bent the corner, instantly landing his eyes on Reishee who leaned comfortably against his Cadillac. Abdullah pulled over and jumped out of the BMW, strolling up to Reishee.

"What's the deal, cousin?" Abdullah chirped.

Reishee smiled. "I got something to show you, but not here," he said, losing his smile. "I'll show you when we get to the Penn," he added, heading to driver's side of the Cadillac.

Abdullah hopped back into the Beemer and waited for Reishee to glide off. Reishee shuttled down the street, and Abdullah followed suit, jumping on his trail. In a matter of minutes, they eased into the housing project known as the Penn.

Simultaneously, Abdullah and Reishee departed their vehicles as Ebony, Trish, and Gwen looked on. Reishee led Abdullah to the rear of his Cadillac.

"Pop the trunk!" Reishee shouted to Gwen.

The trunk sprung open. Instantly, Abdullah's eyes widened in surprise, taking in the sight of Strickland in a fetal position. From that very moment Abdullah's mind traveled to his younger days.

*****

In the small town of Coatesville, Pennsylvania, Abdullah and his mother stood at a counter in a tiny mom-and-pop candy store.

"Hey, little Abdullah, you are getting big. I remember when you were a little ole thing, how old are you?" the caramel-complexioned lady with striking features said warmly, displaying a smile that flaunted dimples.

"I'm seven," Abdullah answered innocently.

"He's the spit of you," the caramel-complexioned lady said gleefully, shooting a look at Abdullah's mother.

Suddenly, a younger Strickland animatedly stepped into the candy shop wielding a .25 revolver. "This ain't for play or show. This is for a stick up, he growled with desperation in his voice, sweating profusely, leveling his firearm on the lady behind the counter.

Immediately, Abdullah's mother stood in front of him, using her body as a human shield as her eyes grew widen from the suspense that lingered in front of her. While her body shivered with the terror that gripped her.

Nervously, the caramel-complexioned lady dug the money out of the cash register while the barrel of Strickland's lethal weapon stared her down.

Petrified out of her mind, the woman from behind the counter handed Strickland the dead presidents.

And just like that, like the drop of a hat, Strickland unloaded a round into the caramel-complexioned lady's temple followed by another round. Followed by another round, all to the store owner's head. She collapsed dead.

With the speed of light, Strickland turned his pistol on Abdullah's mother and repeatedly unleashed bullets into her chest, piercing her with three holes. Breathless, she fell to the floor.

With no mercy in the windows of his eyes, Strickland aimed his firearm directly at the young Abdullah's forehead. Abdullah closed his tear-soaked eyes, preparing to meet the same fate as his mother and the woman store owner, death.

Click! Strickland squeezed, but nothing exited the muzzle of his lethal weapon. *Click!* Strickland squeezed again, but still nothing leaped from the small cannon. Then Abdullah snapped out of the painful wretched memory.

*****

Gwen climbed out of the Cadillac with the butt of a .22 semi-automatic sticking out of the front of her pants, smoothly making her way to Abdullah and Reishee.

"What we gonna do with this clown?" Gwen queried, peering down at Strickland, then glancing at Reishee and Abdullah.

"Bury him. Shiiiiiit, I got the TEC-9 waiting to do its thing. I've dreamed of this day!" Abdullah said solemnly, slightly touching the lethal weapon that sat in his waistband.

"Ab, Strick cleaned himself up. He ain't getting high no more, he getting a little change too. So best believe we gonna get dat paper, if we gotta murder everything related to him to get him to act right, so be it. When everything is said and done, Strick won't be with us," Reishee proclaimed. "Pass off the keys to your dough spots," he added, extending his hand to Strickland.

Minutes in thought, contemplating, Strickland timidly handed Reishee his keys.

"Don't hurt my family, please," Strickland said regretfully and pathetically as his wife and son appeared in his mind.

"How you feel, Strick? You really thought you was gonna get some of this gushy stuff. Didn't you? This is Reishee's pussy. You know what's so sad? This pussy got your dumb ass in dat trunk," Gwen taunted.

"You old fool, we watched your every move for days. Then my girl came at you, and you fell for it, the oldest trick in the book. You dirty old man. If you was loyal to your wiz, we wouldn't be here, would we?" Reishee added his two cents.

"What is he doing? I wonder what's in the trunk. They was glued to it like a bunch of coyotes," Trish said impatiently as she observed Abdullah, Reishee, and Gwen enter a nearby dwelling in the smoky, lusterless, troublesome housing project.

"Who knows? I know he better come on. I can't believe he has us in this drug-infested neighborhood," Ebony replied with frustration in her voice.

Once inside the apartment, Abdullah, Reishee, and Gwen feverishly rambled room to room, ransacking the place.

Moments later, on all fours, Gwen peered under a bed discovering a safe. "I found a safe!" she exclaimed, as she reached under the bed, pulling the chest out.

Abdullah and Reishee rushed into the bedroom to find Gwen hovering over the safe that sat in the middle of the bed.

Aggressively, Reishee fumbled through the keys, seeking for the right one to crack the safe. Within minutes he found the match, smoothly opening the chest.

Simultaneously, viewing the United States currency that rested neatly in the safe, Abdullah's, Reishee's, and Gwen's faces lit up like Christmas trees.

"It's 'bout thirty grand," Reishee estimated.

And with that, the trio slithered out of the apartment with the loot, reverting back to their vehicles, swiftly darting out of the housing project.

As the song "Scenario" by A Tribe Called Quest and Leaders of the New School thumped in the Cadillac. Reishee pushed the vehicle through the dark heartless streets of Chester. Abdullah trailed not far behind his longtime friend with the Geto Boys' "Mr. Scarface" leaping out of the car speakers, with Ebony and Trish completely in the dark to what had been done to what was on the verge of being done transpiring.

Ebony eyed Abdullah intently, while her thoughts ran rampaging in her head, *What is he doing with that gun? Is it for protection? Of course it's for protection. We're up Chester. Abdullah wouldn't hurt anybody, it's just not in him.*

The thought of murder or robbery never crossed Ebony's mind. She knew Abdullah was a lawbreaker, but in her mind, murder and robbery was out of the question. Even though she had a gut feeling that Abdullah was a drug dealer and that was hard as hell for her to swallow. She couldn't imagine him as a cold-blooded murderer. Little did she know.

Trish's mind flashed back to the movie theater when Abdullah professed his love for her. "Trish, can you just listen to what I gotta say? I love you, and I always have from the first time I saw you." Trish smiled ear to ear.

Reishee reared his head out of the Cadillac's driver's side window. "Right here, Abdullah, park here and meet me up there," he directed, gesturing with his hand pointing up the street.

Reishee glided up the block, hooking a right, disappearing around the corner.

"Ab, what are you doing?" Ebony asked as they sat in the parked BMW, while Mary J Blige's "What's the 411" played lightly in the vehicle.

"Just chill for a minute, I'll be right back," Abdullah said soberly, smoothly departing the Beemer.

Quickly, Abdullah trotted up the street, cutting the corner, coming face-to-face with Reishee and Gwen, who was disguised as a crack fiend.

"Check it. She gonna go in the crack house, fronting like she's trying to score. Then we gonna ease our way in and take everything," Reishee informed as he stared down the row home, holding a monstrous facial expression.

*****

67

"Here we go again, Abdullah leaving us in the car. What's around that corner?" Ebony whined. "He's doing something he has no business doing, something criminal I am sure of it. We should pull off and leave his ass up here, I bet he would be steaming," she added as she and Trish erupted in laughter.

*****

Meanwhile, Gwen tapped on the row home's front door. In a matter of minutes, the door swung open, manifesting a tall frail lady whose cheeks were dented in from abusing drugs excessively.

"Whatcha need?" the crack addict sung.

"8 ball," Gwen replied.

"Come in," the crack addict said quickly, inviting Gwen into the dwelling.

Swiftly, Abdullah and Reishee crept up to the crack house. Unhesitatingly, Reishee tossed a key into the front door lock, opening the door. With their lethal weapons drawn, the hoodlums slowly entered the residence. They meticulously moved through the house heading to the rear of the crack house.

Gwen stood next to the frail lady in the back room, in front of a man who sat calmly and collectedly behind a table that was decorated with a heap of packages of street candy along with a .38 Special revolver.

The drug dealer handed Gwen the 8 ball, who in return handed him money.

Nine feet away from the back room in the corridor, Abdullah and Reishee quietly approached. Unexpected to his eyes, the pusher noticed Abdullah and Reishee inching toward him with fire in their eyes, brandishing their lethal weapons.

In a frenzy panic the drug dealer reached for the .38 special revolver that laid on the table. Abdullah and Reishee had the drop, bullets from their guns ripped through the man's head and chest, not giving him the opportunity to squeeze. The pusher plummeted out of his chair, falling into the floor, dead. Gwen swiftly pulled out her firearm smoothly, placing it against the frail lady's temple. *Pop! Pop!* The crack fiend buckled.

And with that, the trio gathered up the street candy that ornamented the table. Reishee snatched up the .38 revolver, then he kneeled over the lifeless drug dealer, rifling through his pockets, extracting two bulky knots of dead presidents.

After wiping down, the table destroying the fingerprints, the trio jetted out of the crack house.

Reishee sailed through the troubled streets of Chester, street after street after street with Abdullah on his heels.

Reishee came upon a stop sign. He stopped, while a man and woman proceeded across the street.

"Look, Reishee!" Gwen exclaimed, hitting his knee, gesturing with her head toward the couple.

Animatedly, Reishee pulled over on the side of the road and jumped out of the Cadillac, stepping into the middle of the street. In a matter of minutes, Abdullah wheeled the BMW behind Reishee's vehicle.

"Ebony, I'll be right back," Abdullah said calmly.

"Why? What the hell are you doing? You're not gonna keep leaving me and Trish in the car, this isn't that kind of party," Ebony barked.

"Chill yo! It ain't no need for you to be bugging. I'm not gonna be dat long. I won't be long," Abdullah replied, before he swiftly exited the Beemer.

Abdullah made his way to Reishee, who stood in the street ruled by anxiety.

"Guess who just fell into our laps?" Reishee said excitedly, peering at the couple who neared the next street.

Abdullah shrugged his shoulders as he displayed a blank facial expression.

Reishee flashed a toothless smile. "York, Strickland's right hand. He's going to one of their spots right now."

"What we waiting for then, let's get the motherfucker!" Abdullah uttered lively.

"Right," Reishee replied, flaunting his pearly whites, turning on his heels, proceeding back to his vehicle with Abdullah in toe.

Reishee slid behind the wheel, while Abdullah dropped into the back seat of the Cadillac.

York and his companion unconsciously slipped out of the law-breaker's sight, converging on to the next street, walking further and further away from the trio.

Reishee took the Cadillac out of park, hooking a left onto the next street. Intently, the threesome's eyes searched for the couple. Shortly thereafter Reishee discovered the pair. "It's on, baby, it's on," he said, locking eyes on the couple who strolled hand in hand.

Quickly, Reishee maneuvered the Cadillac into a parking spot. With a lot of motivation, the hoodlums climbed out of the vehicle, cunningly making their way towards the clueless lovebirds.

"York, let me holler at you for a minute," Reishee said loudly, his voice trembling with zeal.

Still clutching each other's hands, York looked over his shoulder. Then he fully turned around, coming face-to-face with the trio who exhibited icy facial expressions. Immediately, York's counterpart followed suit, spinning around.

Abdullah pointed his TEC to the heavens and nonchalantly fired into the sky. Suddenly, York broke loose from his female companion, hand brace, cowardly dashing off into the night, leaving her alone to fend for herself against the wolf like humans, "No, no, no, no, no, please, please don't hurt me… Please!" the lady howled in dread.

While the lady jumped up and down and screamed hysterically, Abdullah, Reishee, and Gwen looked on with sympathy in their eyes.

Reishee glanced at Abdullah, then he nodded toward his Cadillac before locking eyes with Gwen. "Come on, let's go," he said softly, grabbing Gwen by the arm, pulling her away from the distraught woman.

Reluctantly, Abdullah turned on his heels, sluggishly trailing Reishee and Gwen back to the Cadillac.

Sitting behind the wheel with disgust plastered over his face, Reishee gazed out of the windshield.

"York is a little pussy, he didn't have to go out like dat. What kind of man would leave his girl hanging like dat?" Gwen said dryly from the passenger seat.

"A bitch-ass nigga. He would leave his girl in some shit in a New York minute, dat's what we saw. A bitch-ass nigga," Abdullah said sharply from the back seat.

"York thinks he got ghost on us. I can't wait to see the look on his grill when he steps into the crib and finds us chilling," Reishee said with a smirk, as he took the Cadillac out of park, pulling off.

Moments later, Reishee slid onto a little street, immediately discovering flashing lights, a squad car sitting in front of a row home. "Get down! 5-0! 5-0!" Reishee hollered.

Quickly, Abdullah and Gwen slouched in their seats while Reishee calmly pushed the vehicle pass the two lawmen who sat restfully in the blinking light patrol car.

"Somebody called the police. I bet it was York. We hot now," Reishee proclaimed, letting out a sigh, watching the flashing light squad car from the rearview mirror.

"Yo, park somewhere, so I can handle my business," Abdullah said eagerly, still slouched down.

"Alright, let's handle this y'all can sit up, it's cool it ain't no police around," Reishee replied as he hooked a right onto another street.

*****

Strickland lay on his back, staring at the ceiling of the dark trunk, bracing himself as a single tear dropped out of his eye. He wiped the lone tear away and took a real deep breath. Strickland pictured his wife waiting for him to come home. He envisioned his three-year-old son racing to him with open arms. Then the grim reality struck him; he would never see them again. "Goodbye, Deborah. Goodbye, little Strick. I love y'all," Strickland lamented.

The hood of the trunk popped open, and there stood a glaring Gwen. "Get out of the fucking trunk, you fucking degenerate!" Gwen roared, leveling her firearm at Strickland's dome.

71

Strickland climbed out of the trunk to be greeted by a vacant lot and the baleful smiles of Abdullah and Reishee, who stood on the side of Gwen, a few feet away.

"What are you waiting for, man? Let's get this shit over with. Kill me!" Strickland howled, peering at Abdullah then Reishee.

Simultaneously, baffled by Strickland's arrogance and straight-forwardness, Abdullah and Reishee shot each other looks with disbelief in their eyes.

"I've squeezed the trigger many times, I've killed many times, there's a question you gotta ask yourself," Strickland paused, looking Abdullah, Reishee, and Gwen directly in the eyes one by one, "when the time comes to you and you're staring death in the face, you're on the other side of the gun. How are you gonna take it, how you gonna act? Like a soldier or a coward? See, dat's the question. You see, I'm gonna take it like a soldier, 'cuz it is what it is. I made the wrong move, and y'all got me, so let's do this. Kill me! Kill me!"

Chapter 8

"I wish Ab would hurry the fuck up!" Ebony complained as she stared out of the passenger seat window, where Abdullah was nowhere to be found.

"You're not lying girl, I feel the same way. He needs to bring his butt on," Trish agreed from the back seat.

"Are you kidding me? I do not believe this!" Ebony exclaimed.

"What? What is it?" Trish queried.

"Ab has Jade!" Ebony announced, waving the tape in the air, showing her friend."

"Hey, play it," Trish said softly.

"That's exactly what I'm doing," Ebony replied with a smile, shoving the cassette into the tape deck.

Instantly, Jade's "Don't Walk Away" seeped out of the car radio's speaker, persuading Ebony and Trish to sing along.

*****

Mercilessly, a train of bullets erupted from the muzzle of Abdullah's TEC-9, crashing into Strickland's chest and knocking him on his back while Reishee and Gwen looked on from the sidelines. Abdullah ceased firing his lethal weapon and quickly made his way to Strickland, who lay on his back, with blood pouring out of his wounds.

Now standing over the twisted and stretched-out Strickland, Abdullah viciously kicked his leg. Strickland made no reaction to the fierce kick. At point-blank range, Abdullah nonchalantly dumped a handful of slugs into Strickland's chest. Quickly, Reishee strolled over to Abdullah, and Strickland, whose chest was riddled with bullets, to get a better look at his longtime friend's deed.

"Talk about overkill. Damn," Reishee stated as he viewed the lifeless Strickland.

"Gwen, pop the trunk," Reishee said hurriedly, standing at the rear of his Cadillac accompanied by Abdullah.

Gwen opened the door to the Cadillac and leaned into the vehicle, quickly opening the glove department, pushing the yellow button that sat in the box. And with that the trunk immediately swung open.

"Do you got any trash bags in here?" Abdullah asked, as him and Reishee huddled over the trunk, surveying the box. "I ain't trying to get blood on me," he added.

"You pretty motherfucker. Oh you too pretty to get blood on you, huh?" Reishee teased, chuckling.

"Listen to this, the pretty bol of all pretty bols is calling me a pretty bol," Abdullah retorted, bursting out in laughter.

As Abdullah and Reishee joked around, Gwen abruptly interrupted. "We don't got time for the games. I ain't trying to go to death row, so come on, hurry up, put the bol in the trunk," she barked.

Reishee scooped four trash bags from the trunk, handing Abdullah two. Then they made their way back to the corpse. The hoodlums quickly slipped the trash bags over the stiff. Then the lawbreakers lifted the corpse up off the ground, Abdullah holding the shoulders, Reishee holding the legs. While they transported the body toward the trunk, Gwen scoped out the vacant lot for the authorities and onlookers. Abdullah and Reishee struggled a few minutes with the lifeless Strickland before putting the corpse into the trunk.

"Yo, dat bitch was heavy," said an out-of-breath Reishee, slamming down the lid of the trunk.

We got one more thing to do, and we're home free. And dat's bury the nigga, dat's a piece of cake, dat ain't nuffin, we just gotta get out my mommom's way. We need a licensed driver," Abdullah replied.

Reishee flashed a smile. "Dat's taken care of, we all right. My wife Gwen gots license," he said confidently.

"Oh shit, dat's who you used to talk about all the time when we was in the youth study center," Abdullah said in surprise, realizing who Gwen was.

Instantly, Abdullah's mind traveled back to the time when he was incarcerated with Reishee in the Philadelphia's Juvenile facility.

"Ab, I'm gonna beat the murder rap, watch, remember redhead kingpin? Remember the pump-it hottie cut? The video? I got a girl who look just like one of them girls, word up, she bad, Ab. She loyal, real, she's the truth, you know why she's loyal, real, and the truth?" Reishee said smoothly, in a low tone, while him and Abdullah sat in a mess hall crowded with delinquents.

"Nah, why?" Abdullah replied with a blank facial expression.

"Cuz she got rid of the thing dat could have sent me upstate in the mountains. The witness ain't never stepping into the courtroom, not 'cuz they don't want to, 'cuz they can't. You know what I'm saying? What girl you know would do dat for you?" Reishee said soberly.

"Yo I don't know no girl dat gets down like dat," Abdullah said with a hint of admiration in his voice.

"My lawyer said that without the witness they gotta throw the case out. I'ma just lay back and wait for the good news," Reishee said gleefully.

*****

Gwen pulled up behind the 92 candy apple red BMW 525i. Swiftly, Abdullah climbed out of the back seat of the Cadillac and made his way to the passenger side where Reishee sat calmly.

"Let's get this shit done, y'all just follow me, all right?" Abdullah said before heading toward the parked Beemer.

Gwen backed out from behind the BMW. She slowly maneuvered the black Cadillac alongside the driver's side of the Beemer while Abdullah was just about to open the driver's side door.

"Ab, you want this half pint of Hennessy? Can you handle it? You know you have to drive," Reishee said with a grin.

"How the hell you gonna ask an alcoholic dat?" Abdullah said sarcastically. "You motherfucking right, I want dat Hennessy, pass off," he added.

Abdullah approached Reishee, who sat restfully in the passenger seat. Reishee handed Abdullah the liquor.

"This is for the niggaz who ain't here," Abdullah declared, as he twisted the lid off the bottle, then pouring the liquor on the pavement.

Abdullah took a swig, and instantly the harsh taste furrowed his face. Subsequently, Abdullah reverted back to the BMW. As he flopped into the vehicle, he was greeted with Troop's "I Will Always Love You."

Ebony reached over to the car radio's knob and turned the music down.

"Well, it's about time. What was you doing?" Ebony ranted.

"Girl, I'm a grown man," Abdullah fired back, reaching over to the car radio, turning Troop's "I Will Always Love You" back up.

"You are not a grown man, you are a delusional teenager," Ebony countered, whipping her head side to side, turning the music back down.

They all laughed at Ebony's comment.

Shortly after, Abdullah sailed the '92 candy-apple red BMW 525i out of the city of Chester with Reishee not far behind.

As the lawbreakers traversed on the back zigzag curvy dark roads of Pennsylvania, Abdullah peered into the rearview mirror, planting his eyes on Trish, who looked straight ahead.

Feeling eyes digging into her face, Trish looked up into the rearview mirror, locking eyes with Abdullah, warmly displaying her pearly whites while Slick Rick's, "Teenage Love" leaped from the car-radio speaker.

Ebony sat in the passenger seat, staring out of window with no idea that her best friend and boyfriend were flirting right under her nose.

Then suddenly, Ebony reached over to car radio, turning the music down.

"Are you a drug dealer?" Ebony queried with skepticism in her voice, afraid of what the answer might be.

"Why? Would dat make a difference? Why does it matter?" Abdullah replied, dancing around the question as he kept his eyes on the road.

"I mean you have all this money, you're driving a BMW, you're carrying a gun. Why was you making all them stops? And why the hell was you in jail? Huh?" Ebony rambled.

"Oh my goodness, he has a gun," Trish marveled.

Before Abdullah could reply, Ebony spoke. "Just be honest," she said.

Abdullah sighed. "If it's true, okay, let's say it's true. I'm a drug dealer. You mean to tell me you wouldn't mess with me anymore? If it's like dat, you really don't love me like you say you do, 'cuz regardless of who I am, if you really love me it wouldn't matter," he said pointedly.

"I did not say I would not mess with you anymore. I just want to know who my boyfriend is," Ebony replied cautiously with serious eyes.

"What do you—"

Again, Ebony cut Abdullah off. "Can you please answer my question? Are you dealing drugs?"

"I would if you just give me a chance instead of cutting me off," Abdullah retorted, gulping the liquor from the Hennessy bottle. "No, I don't sale drugs."

"All right, whose car is this? And why was you locked up?" Ebony pestered.

What's up with this girl? She's tripping, Abdullah thought to himself. While he chuckled.

"What, you writing a book?" Abdullah smart-mouthed.

Trish sat back in the rear seat, looking on. She too wondered about Abdullah's lifestyle, but she wasn't about to judge him. To her it really wasn't a factor if he was or wasn't a drug dealer. Trish could not for the life of her ignore the fact that Abdullah professed his love to her.

*****

"Reishee, where are we going?" Gwen inquired as she trailed Abdullah.

"The ville," Reishee responded. From the passenger seat.

"Coasteville?" Gwen said with uncertainty in her voice.

"Yeah," Reishee said softly.

"I got an older sister up that way," Gwen informed, turning her head towards Reishee to get a glance.

"I didn't know you had a sister. I thought you was the only kid," Reishee marveled in surprise.

"I am the only kid concerning my mom's, but my pop has two kids, me and sis," Gwen relayed.

"How old is she?" Reishee pried.

"Twenty-nine," Gwen answered hurriedly.

"Gwen?" Reishee paused then he continued, "You been down with me from the gate, you've proved your loyalty and love, and I love you to death for dat. You're my heart and everything. I would die for you, I swear to God I would," he said sincerely, looking into her face with the glare of love in his eyes.

"Aw, Reishee, you're so sweet. I love you too, baby, there's nothing I wouldn't do for you. Nothing," Gwen said joyously.

"I want a little Reishee. Damn, I can't wait to you have our baby," Reishee declared.

"I can't wait either. I wonder what we're gonna have. It don't matter, though, as long as our baby is healthy," Gwen said gently.

"Eight more months to go, eight months, baby!" Reishee exclaimed as he stared out of the passenger-side window.

*****

"How many times we gotta go through this shit?" Abdullah said with irritation leaping from his voice.

"Why are you getting an attitude?" Ebony fired back.

"'Cuz, I already told you I don't sale drugs," Abdullah roared.

"Fine, I will not ask you anything else anymore," Ebony retorted.

Abdullah sighed. "Ebony, I got the gun for protection. You know them Chester niggaz killed Jax. What I look like being in Chester with no protection? You seen what they did to Jax, they ain't no joke. I ain't going out like dat. The ride is my uncle's," he explained.

"What about the jail thing?" Ebony queried.

"Oh the jail thing. I had gotten pulled over for driving without a license, dat's why I was in lockup," Abdullah answered.

"Abdullah, why do you hang with Reishee?" knowing he's from Chester? One day he might set you up," Ebony said with a suspicious facial expression.

"Listen, I trust Reishee with my life, he would never set me up, he's a loyal cat," Abdullah replied, as he kept his eyes on the road.

Chapter 9

About forty-five minutes later, Abdullah peered into the rearview mirror to discover Trish fast asleep. Abdullah looked over to Ebony and slyly smiled. With one hand on the wheel, Abdullah reached over, grabbing Ebony's hand, resting her fingers onto his Johnson. In a matter of seconds, Ebony aggressively massaged, tugged, and choked Abdullah's manhood.

As Abdullah shoved the BMW through Pennsylvania's back roads, Ebony greeted his Johnson with her plumpish lips, accompanied by her warmish, slippery mouth. Abdullah twitched back in his seat from the sensational slob job he was receiving.

Ebony dipped her head up and down as her jaws clutched Abdullah's manhood. Gradually, increasing speed, moving quicker and quicker. Violently, she slurped and sucked away.

Unexpectedly to Ebony, before she knew it, Abdullah exploded in her mouth. Promptly, Ebony removed her embracing jaws from Abdullah's Johnson while the remainder of his seeds flew onto her cheek. With a silly facial expression, Ebony wiped Abdullah's juices from her face.

In the woods up the road from the '92 candy-apple red BMW 525i, a deer emerged from the sticks. The wild animal roamed in the narrow road while Abdullah drew near, completely unaware of what lay in store.

"Abdullah! Abdullah! What is that up there in the road?" Ebony exclaimed.

"Oh shit!" Abdullah said animatedly, as he wheeled the BMW out of the way of the deer, just missing the wild animal by a few feet.

Abdullah slammed his foot against the brake, putting the Beemer in park, immediately hopping out of the vehicle where farms and barns decorated the scenery. Ebony followed suit. Frantically, the deer dashed across the narrow road disappearing into the night, while the sound of a lone gunshot rang out echoing in the air.

Simultaneously, Abdullah and Ebony turned in the direction where the disturbing noise blossomed to find Gwen behind the trigger accompanied by Reishee, standing by the passenger side of the Cadillac.

The commotion interrupted Trish's beauty sleep, causing her to leap up.

"What the hell is going on?" Trish uttered to herself as she proceeded to climb out of the back seat.

"You missed dat deer, dat bitch was too fast, she got ghost on you," Reishee japed, chuckling.

"I might have gotten dat damn thing, you don't know dat," Gwen fired back, whipping her head side to side.

"Reishee ya wifey ain't nuffin nice," Abdullah proclaimed, laughing and smiling uncontrollably.

"Oh hell no. Take me the hell home. Abdullah, you got me around a bunch of psychos. Take me home!" Ebony demanded.

"What the fuck did you say, bitch?" Gwen barked with a monstrous facial expression.

Ebony paused before she responded, looking Gwen up and down. "I said you're a psycho bitch. Bitch, that's what the fuck I said. I know you heard that loud and clear, didn't you?"

Gwen launched toward Ebony. Swiftly, Abdullah slid in between the pair.

As Ebony and Gwen bickered, Trish quietly crept up from behind with her hands balled up in fists.

"Don't do it, homegirl, don't even try it," Reishee warned.

Stunned by Reishee's body language and the evilness in his eyes, Trish timidly eased back.

"Come on, Ebony and Trish, we out," Abdullah said, grabbing Ebony's arm, escorting her back to the BMW with Trish trailing not far behind.

"Listen, Ebony, you is tripping for real. You stay talking shit," Abdullah chided from behind the wheel of the Beemer.

"I just call it how I see it. You have psychos for friends, plain and simple," Ebony fired from the passenger seat, rolling her eyes.

"My friends ain't no psychos. You need to go 'head with dat bullshit," Abdullah countered, defending his partners in crime. "I'll be back," he said, departing the vehicle.

Abdullah strolled up to Reishee's Cadillac where him and Gwen sat calmly, listening to the song "Head Banger" by EPMD, featuring K-Solo, Redman, Das EFX, and Keith Murray.

Reishee slid down the passenger-side window, adjusting the car radio's volume to a low tone.

"What's up? Is everything cool?" Abdullah asked with sincerity in his voice.

"Yeah everything is cool, we chilling. Ab, me, and Gwen. Ain't worried 'bout dat dumb-ass girl. Shiiiiiiiiiit, we got more things to worry about like the body in the trunk," Reishee said pointedly.

*****

"What happened while I was sleep?" Trish inquired.

"Girl, Abdullah almost hit a deer. Then that thrown-off bitch tried to shoot the poor thing," Ebony related.

"What?" Trish marveled with bulging eyes.

"I'm telling you, Trish, things got really bizarre," Ebony said as she turned around in the passenger seat to face her friend. "Me and the thrown-off bitch was about to fight because I called her a psycho."

"What was Abdullah doing when the psycho was shooting?" Trish queried.

"Absolutely nothing. He did nothing but laugh. You know he thinks he's hard, him and his little criminal friend," Ebony replied.

"I just cannot believe that girl was really shooting at a helpless deer. I mean, shooting—period—is insane. Where did she come from?" Trish said, perplexed.

"I know, right? Where did Abdullah meet these people? They're nuts," Ebony scoffed.

While the two girlfriends laughed and chatted, Abdullah snuck up on the pair, kneeling on the side of the BMW, concealing himself.

Briskly, Abdullah rose up, banging on the windows, startling Ebony and Trish, putting their chatter and laughter to bed.

"I shook y'all up. Huh?" Abdullah teased the frightened two girlfriends, flashing a smile as he flopped into the driver's seat.

"Ha, ha, ha...very funny. You're a clown, you know that?" Ebony said sarcastically.

"Abdullah, you're something else, you're a mess," Trish flirted slyly from the back seat.

"Yo! Listen to this, y'all" Abdullah said, quickly inserting a cassette into the tape deck, discreetly eyeing Trish through the rear-view mirror. "(There You Go) Telling Me No Again" by Keith Sweat bled through the speakers. Quietly, the three adolescents sat while Abdullah pulled off with ease with his partners in crime trailing.

Moments later, looking out of the side of the passenger-seat window, Ebony reflected. She questioned herself: did she really love Abdullah? She was starting to have second thoughts about her relationship with him. Ebony couldn't shake off from her mind the vision of Abdullah clutching a lethal weapon. That vision put her in complete dismay. Ebony wasn't buying the excuses about Abdullah toting a lethal weapon for protection. Even though she tried desperately to give him the benefit of the doubt, the little voice in her head kept nagging her.

Ebony turned to Abdullah and stared hard. *What are you hiding? Something isn't right*, she thought to herself, not taking her eyes off Abdullah while Prince's Diamonds and Pearls "Floated In The Air."

Abdullah felt Ebony's eyes dancing on to his face. "What?" Abdullah said plainly as he kept his focus on the road, drifting through Pennsylvania.

"Nothing," Ebony mumbled, swiftly turning her head, peering out of the passenger-side window.

Trish sat comfortably in the rear seat of the Beemer in dreamland. Her thoughts were filled with her finding somebody to love for life, to be happy, the house with the white fence, the kids and the whole nine yards.

Trish wondered if Abdullah could be the one. After all, he did profess his love to her. So in her mind it was possible that some day they could become an item.

Abdullah, with Ebony and Trish, entered the small town of Coatesville, Pennsylvania, with his partners in crime on his heels. Moments later, the BMW and Cadillac trained up to a pay phone that sat in a gas station.

Anxiously, Abdullah departed the Beemer, leaving the engine running, quickly making his way to the telephone booth, slamming twenty-five cents into the talk machine.

Energetically, Abdullah drummed the numbers, while Ebony, Trish, Reishee, and Gwen looked on from the vehicles.

Ring. Ring. Ring. Ring. Ring. Ring. Ring, the pay phone sang.

"This must be déjà vu. How many times do we have to go through this crap?" Ebony wailed as she watched Abdullah intently. "He's up to something, but what?"

Ring, ring, ring, the pay phone rang.

"Hello?" a scratchy-voiced man answered.

"Yo! It's Abdullah," he declared.

"Abdullah?" the scratchy-voiced man on the other end of the line said in a surprised tone. "What's up? Where are you?"

"Coatesville," Abdullah informed.

"At mommom's?" the man pried.

"Nah I'm over on Lincoln. I'm at the gas station across from the diner. I'm driving a red BM, I need your help. You got a shovel? And I need—"

The man cut Abdullah off. "What do you mean you need a shovel? What's going on?" he queried with slight laughter in his voice.

"I need a spot to handle something." Abdullah paused, before continuing, "I gotta get rid of this trash. You know what I'm saying?"

"All right, give me a minute, all right? And don't do anything stupid." *Click!* The man slammed the telephone in Abdullah's ear without uttering another word.

Slowly, Abdullah brought the receiver from his ear. "Damn, he didn't say bye or nothing," Abdullah said to himself as he frowned.

Chapter 10

From out of nowhere, from out of the darkness of the still night emerged a mysterious '79 white Lincoln Continental Town Coupe with tinted windows. Before Abdullah could blink, the white Lincoln pulled up in front of him.

On alert, Abdullah carefully scoped out the mysterious vehicle in vain. Due to the severity of the tinted windows the identity or the identities of the occupant or occupants were concealed.

The mysterious white Lincoln put Abdullah in a state of jitters. Quickly, Abdullah reached for his TEC-9, only to realize that he had left the lethal weapon in Reishee's Cadillac.

Standing by the telephone booth, Abdullah braced himself for the unknown outcome of the uncertainty.

The driver's side door of the white Lincoln swung open. A minute later, a tall figure stepped out of the automobile. The six-four individual wore a Philadelphia Phillies baseball cap accompanied by a hooded sweatshirt dangling over his eyes and nose, preventing Abdullah from identifying him.

With his heart pounding as if it were a drum, Abdullah held his ground, not moving an inch while the strange man eased near. Abdullah knew he had made a huge mistake by being unarmed, leaving himself vulnerable for the predators of the dark night that lurked in the hazardous, mean, heartless streets.

"Abdullah," the strange man called out. "It's me, Kabu, your big brother," he said, lifting his hat and hoodie, revealing his identity.

What the fuck's wrong with me? I just got done talking to my brother on horn, I'm losing it, Abdullah thought to himself, shaking his head in frustration.

"What? What's up? What's wrong?" Kabu asked his brother as he displayed a puzzled facial expression.

"Ain't shit, I just didn't know who you were at first. You got big as a motherfucker, damn you got big. I ain't gonna lie, when you pulled up in the tinted Lincoln, I thought it might be the stickup bols," Abdullah replied.

"Ab, I told you I was on my way, you should've known it was me. All the dirt you've done out here, it's got you paranoid, and dat ain't good, you gotta be easy, I've been home for a month and half now. When you come home?" Kabu said soberly.

"Three days ago," Abdullah relayed.

"It's been years since we been home at the same time. Either I'm doing a bid, or you're doing a bid. It's good dat you're home, though," Kabu said blissfully, embracing his brother tenderly.

The brothers unlocked their embrace.

"Ab, what's the deal? Where's the trash?" Kabu inquired.

"It's in the Caddy," Abdullah informed, pointing in the direction of the black Cadillac where Reishee and Gwen sat comfortably.

"Who is it?" Kabu pried.

"Strickland," Abdullah divulged as sadness and rage gripped his being.

In that instant, Kabu's eyes widened. "Strickland?" he said in astonishment, swallowing hard, clenching his teeth.

"Here's what we're gonna do: chop him up into pieces and spread him all over Pennsylvania, Lancaster, York, Downington, West Chester, I mean all over. We're gonna bury his head right here in the ville, the police won't know shit. It will be a puzzle to them pigs if they do find a body part, but they won't be able to put it together."

Calmly, Abdullah nodded to the coldness that dwelled in his brother's eyes.

"Who is that?" Ebony blurted, as she intently watched the brothers.

"Probably one of Abdullah's jailhouse buddies. I must say, though, he's very tall and nice looking," Trish replied.

"You like him, Trish? I could ask Abdullah to hook the two of you up," Ebony said hurriedly.

"No, I am fine, he's just not my type. Besides, I already have my eyes on somebody else," Trish fired back.

"Who?" Ebony said lively, spinning around in the passenger seat to face her friend.

"For me to know and for you to find out," Trish wisecracked, rolling her neck.

Ebony shot Trish a facial expression that read "Oh no she didn't, you didn't just say that to me," then she burst into a fit of laughter.

Brightly, Trish smiled at her best friend. "Girl, I'm only playing, but I have decided to move on. I'm over Jax. I'm waiting for that special one to come along," she said, looking away from Ebony.

"You know something? I don't think me and Abdullah is gonna work out. He's acting real shady. Do you really think he's carrying that gun for protection? 'Cause personally I don't really believe him. He's hiding something, Trish, I'm sure of it," Ebony said shakily, letting out a sigh.

"Eb, I think you're just jumping to conclusions. Them guys from Chester killed Jax, and we were up in Chester. Suppose them same guys that murdered Jax saw Abdullah? They would have certainly tried to kill him too. I don't blame Abdullah for arming himself," Trish said firmly.

Chapter 11

Ebony sucked her teeth. "Well, you do have a point, but remember I cried when I didn't hear a word from Abdullah. You saw how depressed I was. I wanted to die, that's how bad I felt. I wanted him to call so bad, but he didn't, not one single time. It was like he just vanished off the face of the earth. Now he pops back up in my life like everything is fine. As much as I hate to say this, I don't think I love Abdullah anymore. I must come to terms of letting him go, as hard as that may be. I got to, I don't want any part of his lifestyle," Ebony said sadly, her voice quavering with emotion, while a tear dropped out of her eye, racing down her face.

"For real? You're quitting Abdullah?" Trish said as her eyes bulged with disbelief.

"Um-huh," Ebony replied, moving her head up and down.

"But I thought you really loved Abdullah?" Trish said perplexedly.

"I thought I did too. It's like my love for Abdullah is fading," Ebony said in grief as the tears poured.

"So when are you gonna tell him it's over?" Trish queried, searching her best friend's eyes.

Ebony wiped the tears from her face and took a deep breath. "I don't know. I don't know how to tell him, and honestly I don't think he would actually care if I quit him or not," she said unhappily.

"Why don't you stick it out with Abdullah? Try to work it out with him. Relationships always have their ups and down. They are at times rocky, and things never stay the same. They change, and Abdullah can change. Just hold on to him, listen to your heart," Trish persuaded while she concealed her true feelings for Abdullah.

"You know what? Maybe I should try to work out our relationship, huh? Trish, I'm so confused though, I don't really want to let

Abdullah go. I just can't take all the damn drama. Him carrying guns, that crazy girl shooting, his reckless behavior, his lack of regard for the law. And to put the icing on the cake, he's hiding something, I know he is," Ebony fired back.

"What could he possibly be hiding?" Trish retorted, displaying a solemn facial expression.

"I don't know, but I feel it in my gut, I feel it. Something isn't right with him,"

"What do you mean something isn't right with him?" Abdullah interrupted Ebony as he, along with his brother, encountered the passenger side of the BMW.

"You all in the Kool-Aid and don't even know the flavor," Trish smart-mouthed.

Abdullah smiled at Trish's sarcasm.

"You're something else," he mimicked Trish, gazing at her. "This is my brother Kabu."

"Hi, Kabu," Ebony and Trish chorused.

"Which one of y'all go with my little brother," Kabu pried with furrowed eyebrows.

"Why? I do," Ebony said quickly.

"Chill, sweet thing," Kabu said with a smile as held his hands in the air. "I don't want no problems. I'm just checking on my fam. Dat's my little brother, you know? I'm just concerned 'bout who he mess with."

Moments later, Reishee strolled up to Abdullah and his brother while Ebony and Trish sat comfortably in the BMW while Gwen looked on from the Cadillac.

Abdullah introduced Reishee to Kabu. The two strangers greeted each other with firm handshakes.

*****

Kabu lounged behind the wheel of his Lincoln where Abdullah sat shotgun, along with Reishee occupying the back seat.

"I got a spot up east end. Ab, take the girls up mommom's. Who's the chick in the caddy?" Kabu said smoothly.

"Dat's my wifey," Reishee informed.

"Is dat right?" Kabu said plainly.

"She's straight," Abdullah vouched.

"Do she know about the body?" Kabu queried.

"Do she know about the body? She the one who kidnapped the joker," Abdullah exclaimed.

"Cool," Kabu said calmly, peering through windshield.

Chapter 12

In a decent neighborhood, Abdullah floated the BMW into an alley that sat in between backyards. After parking, Abdullah cut the engine off and turned toward Ebony, who hawkeyed him keenly.

"What? Why are you looking at me like dat?" Abdullah questioned with a hint of irritation in his voice.

"I'm looking at you like that because I am tired of you leaving us in the car while you do what Lord knows what. I'm sick of it. I'm sick of it, Abdullah," Ebony replied angrily, sitting tensely in the passenger seat with crossed arms.

"Can you just chill? You is bugging, dat's my mommom's crib," Abdullah said as he pointed to the modest house that rested in front of the backyard they sat in front of in the wholesome neighborhood. "I want you to meet her. Is dat all right with you?"

"Well, yeah, I guess so," Ebony fired back with an attitude.

"Come on, Eb, why you acting like dat?" Abdullah whined.

Abdullah, Ebony, and Trish departed the '92 candy-apple red BMW 525i while they made their way into the dark yard. They were greeted by an indistinguishable shadowy shotgun-toting figure.

"Who there?" the man inquired, as he aimed his rifle in the direction of the trio.

Immediately, Abdullah recognized the voice of the man grasping the lethal weapon.

"It's Abdullah!" he declared hysterically.

"Boy, do you know what time of the night it is? And you out here sneaking around, you was finning to get your damn head blown off," the man ranted.

"Poppop, I was gonna use the back door 'cuz I didn't want to wake y'all up..."

"Bullshit!" Abdullah's grandfather stopped him in his tracks. "Come here, let me see who you got there with you," the elderly man demanded.

Abdullah took a hold of Ebony's arm, gently escorting her toward his grandfather, who stood outside of the house light's beam. Trish followed suit, rubbing shoulders with her best friend Ebony.

With his eyes absorbing the young beauties, Abdullah's grandfather grinned admiringly. "You slick little buzzard you," he said excitedly.

Leading the way, Abdullah's grandfather entered the house with the adolescents close to his heels.

Moments later, Ebony and Trish sat on a couch in the living room watching the television while Abdullah and his grandfather stood near the living room's door passageway.

"Where's mommom?" Abdullah asked.

"Abdullah, you know damn well she's in bed, look at the time," Abdullah's grandfather said sarcastically. "What the hell are you up to?" he added as he squinted.

"Nothing. I ain't up to nothing. It's only going on twelve, pop-pop," Abdullah replied.

"I wasn't born yesterday, ya hear? Your little ass is up to no good… Come here, let me talk to you," Abdullah's grandfather fired back, gesturing his hand toward the next room.

The elderly man stepped into the dining room with his grandson on his trail.

*****

Reishee dropped the lid of the trunk to the Cadillac and proceeded to follow Kuba, who strolled to the backyard of his safe house. The rays of the house light beamed down on to the two shovels that leaned against the safe house.

Snatching up a shovel, Kabu signaled for Reishee to grab the other one. Reishee complied, and they swiftly reverted back to their vehicles.

Gwen lolled behind the wheel of the Cadillac, ear soaking the sound of Boyz II Men's "End of the Road" as her lover with shovel in hand entered the automobile.

"Where's mine at?" Gwen asked.

"Kabu only had two, Gwen," Reishee replied calmly, peering into her pretty brown eyes.

"What we waiting for?" I'm ready to bury this clown," Gwen exclaimed

"We were waiting on Abdullah, he won't be long. Be cool, baby," Reishee expounded, slightly smiling.

Kabu lay back in his Lincoln. Briefly, his mind flashed back to him being released from SCI in Graterford, Pennsylvania. Happily and eagerly, Kabu stepped out of the enormous walls of the gloomy penitentiary into the sunlight to be greeted by fresh air and freedom of the world.

*****

"Which one is your girlfriend?" Abdullah's grandfather queried with a facial expression that read "I know what you're up to."

"The chocolate one is my girl," Abdullah replied, glancing at Ebony and Trish while they quietly sat side by side on the couch, locking eyes on the idiot box.

"All right now, I'm going upstairs. I know you don't want me around. I was young long ago, and let me tell you, back in my day I was sharpie sharp," the elderly man proclaimed, turning on his heels, strutting away.

While Abdullah's grandfather toed up the stairs, Abdullah commenced to go through the house as if he were a cat burglar. Slowly, Abdullah entered a garage. Instantly, his eyes come upon a saw and shovel that rested on a shelf. And with that, Abdullah grabbed the saw and shovel, rushing back to the BMW, throwing the saw and shovel on to the rear floor of the vehicle. Moving like he was on pins and needles, not being detected, Abdullah slipped back into the garage to find a chainsaw.

The sight of the chainsaw lounging on the shelf brought a wicked smile upon Abdullah's face. Promptly, Abdullah snatched up the powerful toll. Unhesitatingly, Abdullah eased his way up out of the house without being noticed by Ebony and Trish. Abdullah climbed into the Beemer, placing the chainsaw onto the passenger seat, gently and quietly, pulling the driver's side door close, speeding off into the night.

Chapter 13

Half past midnight, Abdullah pulled up in front of his brother's safe house where the lawbreakers sat restfully in their vehicles: Kuba in his Lincoln, Reishee in his Cadillac accompanied by Gwen.

Abdullah stepped out of the BMW discreetly, clutching the chainsaw, shaking his head up and down. "Let's get this show started," he said plainly.

Simultaneously, the doors of the Cadillac and Lincoln swung open. Quickly, Kuba and Reishee departed their automobiles, eagerly making their way to the trunk of the Cadillac.

"Pop this shit, Gwen," Reishee ordered, as he cupped his hands underneath the trunk.

The trunk leaped open, and Kuba leaned over the hatch, simply grabbing the corpse and tossing the body over his shoulder proceeding to the house with Abdullah trailing not far behind. Reishee eased his way to Gwen, who climbed out of the Cadillac.

Hovering above Strickland's lifeless body in the middle room of the safe house, Abdullah pushed the blade of the chainsaw against his neck. Blood gushed from Strickland's cervix, like a faucet. The steel sunk deeper and deeper into his flesh, ultimately severing his head.

Shortly after, Kabu stepped into the room holding a chainsaw and bedsheets. Swiftly and aggressively, he chopped away Strickland's hands.

*****

"Abdullah, Abdullah," Ebony muffled, her eyes searching the next room for her boyfriend, while she sat on the couch. Ebony turned to face Trish to find her intently observing the idiot box.

Ebony hopped off the couch and tiptoed into the next room to get a clearer look. She surveyed the dining room where Abdullah was nowhere in sight. Shaking her head in disbelief and disgust, Ebony hustled back into the living room, flopping on to the couch.

*****

Reishee and Gwen entered the bleakish house to discover the two brothers dismantling Strickland's body. Upon landing their eyes on the couple, the two siblings ceased their butchery.

"Yo, pretty bol, there's a saw in the BM on the floor," Abdullah proclaimed.

"Join us," Kabu added his two cents, as he grasped the chainsaw with an inhumane facial expression.

Not saying a word, Reishee and Gwen darted out of the bleakish safe house to retrieve the saw. Within minutes the pair returned back to the blooded room where the two brothers artfully performed their unthinkable act.

Reishee joined in on the deed, pressing the tooth of the saw against Strickland's knee, commencing to moving the blade back and forth.

Initially, Reishee struggled to drive the saw through Strickland's flesh, but within a few strokes he quickly got the hang of it.

Moments later, while Reishee voraciously drove the saw through Strickland's leg, Gwen callously, put Strickland's head into a pillow-case, then a trash bag.

*****

Kabu wheeled his '79 white Lincoln Continental Town Coupe with tinted windows onto the side of a dark dirt deserted stretch of a road where the scenery of woods rested not far behind. Calmly, Abdullah sat in the passenger seat with a stronghold of a trash bag.

In a matter of seconds appeared Reishee and Gwen. Gwen maneuvered the Cadillac to the rear of the Lincoln.

The lawbreakers climbed out of their vehicles and made their way in to the murky woods. Now standing in a huddle with Abdullah, Reishee, and Gwen in the depths of the woods, Kabu plunged a shovel into the ground, swiftly digging up the soil from the earth's floor, developing a hole.

"See how fast I made dat jawn?" Kabu vaunted, peering down on the cavity in the ground.

Abdullah reached inside the garbage bag, pulling out a pillowcase. Then Abdullah extracted Strickland's head from the pillowcase, gazing at the emptiness in his eyes, gazing at the haunting and chilling look of death. Abdullah dropped the lifeless head into the shallow pit. Immediately, Kabu covered Strickland's head with dirt.

Abdullah and Kabu traversed to the neighboring county of Coatesville, Lancaster, while Reishee and Gwen proceeded to Downingtown another county in Pennsylvania.

Standing in the woods several feet away from a cliff that sat above a creek, hovering over a shallow makeshift grave, Kabu tossed dirt over Strickland's torso. While Abdullah waited in the Lincoln fifty yards away alongside a long, narrow, unoccupied roadbed.

Moments later, Kabu returned to his vehicle. "You all right, Ab?" he asked after falling into his seat at the wheel looking straight ahead.

Abdullah let out a sigh, turning to face his brother. "I'm cool," he replied.

"I don't know, after we chopped Strickland up, you seemed different, shaky," Kabu said.

"I'm thinking about Mom, I miss her. Damn I miss her," Abdullah said with sadness in his eyes.

"I know, I miss Mom too. Ab, the pain ain't never gonna go away. We just learn to live with it. I've killed Strick a thousand times in my mind. I thought when he was dead and gone the pain would be gone, but pain is still in my cold heart. The pain ain't never gonna leave us until we're gone," Kuba said grievously.

"The pain is gonna be here until we're dead," Abdullah said dryly, looking on as if he was in a trance.

"Are you going back down Delaware later on?" Kabu queried as he pulled off with ease while the "Mind of a Lunatic" by the Geto Boys slightly leaped from the car system.

"Yeah I gotta take Ebony and Trish back. I know they want to go home. I'll be back tomorrow though," Abdullah answered.

"Tomorrow is good. Listen, I need you to handle something with me. We gonna do this together," Kabu said soberly, turning up the volume of his car radio to the max.

As Kabu pushed his '79 white Lincoln Continental Town Coupe through the state of Pennsylvania, he and his brother rode in complete silence, simply listening to the sounds of the Geto Boys.

Kabu parked in back of the '92 candy apple-red BMW 525i.

"All right, Abdullah, I'll see you tomorrow, As-Salaam-Alaikum," Kabu said as his brother climbed out of his vehicle, then he rocketed the Lincoln down the street.

When Abdullah pulled up in front of his grandmother's house, he was greeted by the chirping birds.

Calmly, Abdullah headed to the front door of his grandmother's house. Before Abdullah could push his key into the lock of the front door, the door swung open, and there stood his grandmother with open arms, smiling and embracing him.

"How's my boy?" Abdullah's grandmother asked.

"I'm fine, mommom," Abdullah replied.

Abdullah followed his grandmother in to the house. The aroma from his grandmother's breakfast filled the air.

As Abdullah made his way into the living room, he scanned the room, immediately noticing that Ebony and Trish were not on the couch where he had left them the night before.

Abdullah's heart dropped in bewilderment. *Where they at? Did they go home?* he thought to himself, staring at the couch in a trance-like state.

"Abdullah! Abdullah! Come eat your breakfast before it gets cold, come and get it," Abdullah's grandmother summoned in a loud tone.

Abdullah's grandmother's hollering instantly snapped him out of his trancelike state. Abdullah stepped into the dining room to be taken by total surprise, discovering Ebony and Trish sitting snugly at the dining-room table with his grandparents.

"Ebony, can you pass the syrup please?" Abdullah's grandmother said in a very pleasant manner as she warmly smiled at Ebony.

Ebony handed Abdullah's grandmother the bottle of syrup, and then she turned to Abdullah. "Well, what are you waiting for? Have a seat," she smart-mouthed.

Everybody laughed with the exception of Abdullah, who didn't find Ebony's pushy comment funny at all.

Abdullah pulled out a chair and proceeded to have a seat right next to Ebony. As Abdullah got situated, he felt eyes digging into his face. He looked up then went across the table to find Trish behind the intense stare, sitting across from Abdullah, downing her pancakes. Trish recurrently eyed Abdullah as if she was trying to tell him something with her hinting eyes.

Abdullah's grandfather peered at Trish then he glanced at his grandson. A half-smile formed on the elderly man's face as he observed the flirting between Abdullah and Trish, who underhandly played eye tag.

"Abdullah, since you been home, have you seen your brother?" Abdullah's grandmother inquired with a curious look on her face.

"Yes, mommom, I was with him last night," Abdullah replied, slicing his pancakes, gliding a piece of a hotcake into his mouth.

"I hope y'all was behaving y'all selfs. Abdullah, you only been out of the slammer for four days now. Don't you dare go back! The next time you see Kabu, you tell him to come by the house. We gonna eat together as a family, shoot, he hasn't been by here since you been home Abdullah," the elderly woman said with a hint of disappointment in her voice.

Meanwhile, miles away in sunny Philadelphia, Pennsylvania. Reishee frantically tore through the streets of brotherly love along with Gwen riding shotgun with a brigade of police vehicles in hot pursuit of them. Street after street after streets, corners after corners, stop signs after stop signs, red light after red light. Through the boulevard, through Kelly drive to '76, eventually coming upon the Ben

Franklin Bridge where the authorities occupied a roadblock stationed deep within the bridge, waiting patiently.

Realizing that they were trapped, Gwen took Reishee's hand into hers, gripping him tightly as sadness and doom invaded the windows of her eyes.

Now yards away from the roadblock with a mass of firearms and rifles leveled at the Cadillac. Reishee stopped, putting the vehicle in park. Reishee took a long deep breath, as did Gwen. Swiftly, the wanted pair stepped out of the Cadillac where the muzzles of deadly weapons the authorities clutched stared them down.

"Surrender peacefully. Put your hands in the air," the lawman with the bullhorn instructed, standing in the midst of the roadblock behind a police cruiser.

Sadly, Reishee smiled at Gwen as he took a hold of her hand. Slightly trembling, Gwen returned a smile to the love of her life while grief and fear masked her face.

"I love you, Reishee," Gwen declared with her voice cracking with emotion.

"I love you," Reishee replied firmly.

Abruptly, the thuggish couple bolted, making their way to the edge of the bridge as the authorities briefly froze looking on in astonishment and disbelief.

"Don't jump, don't jump, we can figure this out," the lawman with the bullhorn exclaimed, while he and his colleagues feverishly raced toward the apparent suicidal pair.

Standing on the towering ledge of the Ben Franklin Bridge, Reishee slowly reached out for Gwen's hand while she extended her hand to his. Zealously and passionately, their hands grasped, intensely, their eyes connected as they hopelessly uttered, "I Love You" to one another. Then they leaped from the imposing bridge.

*****

West Chester, Pennsylvania, sometime later, Abdullah along with Ebony and Trish wheeled the BMW into a McDonald's restaurant parking lot.

"What are you doing? Why are you stopping? Take me the hell home," Ebony roared from the passenger seat.

"Chill, just give me a minute. I need to holler at Reishee, it will only take a second," Abdullah said hurriedly, as he cut the engine off, climbing out of the vehicle.

Abdullah anticipated that Reishee and Gwen would be in the parking lot waiting, but as far as his eyes could see they were nowhere in sight.

Five minutes passed by, then ten, then twenty. Shortly after a half hour, still no trace of the thugged-out couple.

"Abdullah, you said a minute. It has been thirty-five minutes. Reishee isn't coming. He would have been here by now," Ebony expounded while she stuck her head out of the passenger-side window.

"He'll be here!" Abdullah shouted, standing twenty feet away from the '92 candy-apple red BMW 525i.

With two hours well gone, Abdullah refused to sweat, still patiently waiting for his partners in crime while Ebony and Trish eyeballed him.

"Here it is two hours later and he's still waiting like a damn fool," Ebony said with an attitude.

"I know, what is his problem?" Trish said from the back seat as she and Ebony stared Abdullah down.

Shaking her head, Ebony exhaled sharply. "I really don't know what to do with Abdullah. A part of me wants to let go, but I can't. I can't picture him with anybody else, you know? I would be so hurt to see him move on with somebody. Especially if it was somebody I know," she said soberly.

"Wow, I know you have deep feelings for Abdullah." Trish paused, then she continued, "But I had no idea it was that serious."

Trish's mind started to race. She couldn't but help but wonder if Ebony was sending her a little hint not to get entangled with Abdullah. She questioned her being. Was it worth jeopardizing her and Ebony's friendship for Abdullah?

"Trish, Trish, Trish," Ebony called her best friend's name.

"Huh?" Trish replied, lost in thought.

"Are you okay? Relax a little, you look real tense, like you're worried about something. What's on your mind?" Ebony said while she turned around in the passenger seat facing Trish, looking her dead square in the face.

"Girl, I'm fine," Trish retorted, flaunting a counterfeit smile.

"I'm so sorry, it's Jax you're thinking about. I don't know what I would do if Abdullah was murdered, I really couldn't imagine it," Ebony said with sympathy in her eyes.

Ebony's words instantly turned Trish's counterfeit smile into a frown.

"Why must you bring Jax up? Why did you have to go there? And yes I was thinking about Jax. I don't think I will ever stop, but I got to move on as hard as it may be," Trish fired back, lying through her teeth as she looked away from her best friend.

"I didn't mean it like that, Trish. you know I'm here for you. If you ever need to talk, I am here. I'm your girl, that's what friends are for," Ebony said with a heartfelt smile.

"Let's leave," Trish suggested playfully.

"Are you serious?" Ebony questioned as she glanced at the key that rested in the ignition.

"No, I'm just kidding," Trish said, beaming uncontrollably.

"Are you sure? Because we can leave this jailbird right here, right now," Ebony howled, bursting into a fit of laughter.

Chapter 14

Smoothly, Abdullah entered the first state accompanied by Ebony and Trish. As he whipped the BMW through Claymont, Delaware, his pager started to vibrate. With one hand on the wheel, Abdullah extracted his loot clocker from his pocket. Ebony shot Abdullah a look that read "It better not be a no, girl." Unexpectedly, within a blink of an eye, Ebony snatched Abdullah's beeper from his hand before he could finish reading the numbers that furnished the screen.

"What do we have here?" Ebony japed as she peered on the number that decorated the face of the pager.

"Stop playing with me, give me my beeper," Abdullah said anxiously as he kept his eyes on the road.

"No! I'll give it to you when you tell me who it is. So what's it gonna be? Who's paging you?" Ebony fired back.

"It's Kabu," Abdullah retorted, as he pulled over in front of Ebony's town house.

"How you know? You didn't have enough time to see the whole number. Your eyes are not that fast," Ebony contested.

"He said he was gonna call—"

Ebony cut Abdullah off. "Fine, take your damn pager," she ranted, throwing the loot clocker at Abdullah, swiftly departing the BMW. "Call me Trish," she added, slamming the door shut, not saying a single word to Abdullah, storming off into her town house.

"Looks like it's just you and me now," Abdullah said jovially as he spun around in the driver seat to face Trish.

And with that, Trish climbed out of the back seat and hopped into the front seat.

"I gotta make a real quick stop before I drop you off. Is dat all right with you?" Abdullah said quickly, searching Trish's eyes, then focusing his eyes on the road pulling off.

"Are you serious? Or do you just want to spend some quality time with me all alone?" Trish queried in a suspicious tone, smiling ear to ear.

"I'm dead serious. Listen, Trish, I still feel the same way about you. I love you, and damn right I want to spend some quality time with you. You're all I think about," Abdullah proclaimed as he jumped onto the highway.

"But what about Ebony? You know how she feels about you? She loves you so much," Trish said softly while she eyed Abdullah.

"I don't know about all dat. You seen how she just acted. She didn't say bye or nuffin'. She didn't say shit. She said bye to you, though. Yo, why are we even talking about her? I don't love her, I love you," Abdullah said sharply, as he occasionally glanced at Trish flooring the '92 candy-apple red BMW 525i through traffic.

"We're talking about her because she's my best friend, that's why," Trish retorted with a concerned facial expression.

"She's your best friend. Look, Trish, I'm tired of playing these games. Just tell me dat you don't feel nothing for me. Can you even tell me dat you don't have any feelings for me? Can you?" Abdullah said fervently.

"No comment," Trish fired back, avoiding Abdullah's questions, peering out of the passenger-side window.

In that instant it became clear as day to Abdullah that Trish wanted him in her world.

"Trish, you don't have to pretend anymore. You don't have to front, it's all about you now. I'm done with Ebony, it's over between us," Abdullah said openly.

"Are you just saying this now because you're with me?" Trish asked coyly.

"I'm saying it 'cuz I mean it, Trish. I mean it," Abdullah said hurriedly.

"I am not gonna lie, Abdullah, you do make me feel a certain way. I actually never knew you cared about me so deeply," Trish said as she gazed at Abdullah, who looked straight ahead on to the freeway.

"Now you know, you probably thought I was bullshitting at the movies. Huh? Listen, Trish, I need you for real," Abdullah said solemnly.

"What do you mean by that, Abdullah? Explain that to me, please," Trish said in a soft, gentle voice.

"I breathe for you, I eat for you, I sleep and wake up for you. I can't live without you. You're the one... I want to grow old with you. I want you to have my babies, you know, a family. You just don't know what I'll do to make you my girl. You just don't know how much I love you," Abdullah declared.

"Abdullah, I really don't know what to say," Trish said, flabbergasted.

"Say we're gonna be together. Say, Abdullah, I'm your girl," Abdullah suggested.

"Boy, you're really one of a kind. You're something else, you're crazy," Trish said, displaying her pearly whites.

"Yeah I'm crazy, crazy about you," Abdullah clarified. "Check this out," he added, throwing a tape into the tape deck.

Keith Sweat's "There You Go Telling Me No Again" engulfed the Beemer as Abdullah maneuvered the vehicle toward the city of Wilmington.

*****

Wilmington, Delaware
Moments later, Abdullah pulled over on the side of a Chinese store on Twenty-Eighth Street.

"I'll be right back," Abdullah said as he affectionately grabbed Trish's chin.

Briskly, Abdullah hopped out of the BMW, making his way to the rear of the Asian establishment where a dumpster rested.

Abdullah reached under the dumpster, seizing a German Walther PPK, tucking the firearm into his waistband. From behind the dumpster stood a lone muscle-bound teenager watching Abdullah's every move, nonchalantly puffing on a blunt.

Abdullah looked up, locking eyes with the muscle-bound teen. Immediately Abdullah smiled just as the muscle-bound teen did, who trotted toward him.

"Vic," Abdullah said as he nodded at his longtime friend.

"What's up, G? I thought dat was you!" Vic said, handing Abdullah the doobie he was puffing on.

"Chilling yo," Abdullah replied, inhaling and exhaling the marijuana.

"What's been going down? I see you creeping. I seen you grab the heater, you slick motherfucker," Vic exclaimed as he passed a forty to Abdullah.

"It ain't 'bout nuffin. I just gotta stay packing, you know what I'm saying?" Abdullah retorted, as he took a long swig of the beer.

Beep, beep, beep, beep, beep, beep, beep, beep, Abdullah's pager alarmed repeatedly.

"Yo, Vic, I'll get up with you later on black. I'm out," Abdullah said energetically, shaking his longtime friend's hand, darting back to the Beemer where Trish sat patiently listening to Keith Sweat's "How Deep Is Your Love."

Abdullah flopped back into the driver's seat, peering deep into the windows of Trish's eyes. "I'm sorry, baby, I didn't mean to take dat long," he said smoothly.

"Don't worry, Ab. It's okay," Trish replied, while she kept her eyes locked with Abdullah's.

"You hungry? Let's get something to eat," Abdullah said gently.

"I thought you would never ask," Trish fired back merrily.

*****

And from that day everything changed for Abdullah. The girl he had longed for and wanted desperately was finally in his grasp, right where he wanted her. Abdullah's dreams were starting to come true, and he refused to let anything or anyone stop them from being real.

"What do you want?" Abdullah queried, glancing at Trish as they stepped into a sub shop that decorated Market Street.

"Okay, let me see," Trish said comfortably, her eyes surveying the menu. "I want a small turkey sub with everything on it, potato chips, and a ginger ale," she added.

"May I help you?" the light-skinned lady with freckles sung in a friendly tone from behind the counter.

"Yeah, give me one small turkey sub with everything on it and a large turkey sub with a lot of mayonnaise, pickles, hot peppers, sweet peppers, two bags of potato chips, a ginger ale and root beer soda," Abdullah said jovially.

Moments later, Abdullah and Trish stepped out of the sub shop, encountering a vigorous foot chase. Three men tore past the pair, racing down the street with a gang of police men in pursue of them. The thugs bent the corner at Twenty-Eighth and Market Street, disappearing out of Abdullah and Trish's view. The uniformed policemen followed suit, converging around the corner. Abdullah looked at Trish and shrugged his shoulders while a smile lit up his face.

By the time Abdullah and Trish made their way around the corner, the hoodlums and lawmen were gone nowhere to be found.

With the quickness, Abdullah pulled off Twenty-Eighth Street as Trish watched him like a hawk.

"Ab, what are we going to do? I like you I really do, but I don't want to hurt my best friend," Trish said with concern in her voice.

"Check this out, we don't tell her nothing. She don't gotta know shit for real. For real, this can be our secret," Abdullah replied while he kept his eyes on the city streets of Wilmington.

Claymont, Delaware

In the midst of a middle-class suburb where lawns were a lively green neatly manicured, where driveways were lined with garages and basketball hoops, where backyards flaunted swimming pools. Abdullah slid in front of Trish's house, turning off the engine to the BMW. Abdullah peered deep into the eyes of the girl he was in love with. He wished he could read her mind as she gazed back at him, smiling lightly.

Intently, the pair stared at each other for a handful of minutes without uttering a single word before Trish broke the silence.

"So this is it, huh?" Trish said naively, while she slowly pushed the passenger side door open.

"No, no this ain't it. I'm gonna call you later on," Abdullah assured.

"Well, okay call me then," Trish said as she smiled ear to ear, moving her head up and down. "Bye, Abdullah," she added, departing the vehicle.

Mesmerized by Trish's intense beauty, Abdullah watched her stroll to her front doorstep. Before Trish vanished in to her residence, she looked back at Abdullah.

Abdullah turned the '92 candy-apple red BMW 525i back on and sped off. Repeatedly, Abdullah's mind flashed with visions of Trish's face as he missiled the BMW down the highway with NWA's "Appetite For Destruction" blaring. Abdullah's pager quavered in his pocket. He assumed it was Ebony while he swiftly extracted his loot clocker from his jean shorts. And sure enough, it was Ebony.

*****

Abdullah sailed into an upscale neighborhood, parking in front of a mini mansion. Slowly, Abdullah climbed out of the Beemer to be greeted by a man who was six feet tall and holding a toothpick shape displaying a pinkish-reddish complexion along with salt-and-pepper hair. He was in his forties.

Chapter 15

"What's the deal, guy? I paged you like a hundred times," the man with the pinkish-reddish complexion said sarcastically as he laughed.

"I was taking care of something," Abdullah retorted, "What's up, Daniel?"

"I got something to show you, little buddy," Daniel proclaimed, leading Abdullah inside his home.

"Aye, Daniel, let me use your horn," Abdullah said plainly as Daniel closed the door behind them.

"Sure, kid, go head. I'll be right back," Daniel said hurriedly, vanishing without a trace into his residence.

Abdullah entered the plush living room where he grabbed a cordless telephone from the telephone cradle, drumming the number.

Ring, ring, ring, ring, ring.

"Hello?" Ebony answered, sitting on a bed in her bedroom.

"Ebony, what's up?" Abdullah said animatedly.

"I really don't know how to say this," Ebony said as her voice cracked with emotion.

"Say what? What are you talking about?" Abdullah exclaimed.

"I'm talking about us, this relationship. I love you, Abdullah, Lord knows I do, but"—Ebony paused as tears started to pour down her face—"I got to let you go."

"All right it's cool, see you," Abdullah fired back callously, hesitating to disconnect the cordless telephone.

"Abdullah, you don't care? You're not hurt?" Ebony asked perplexed.

"It's cool, Ebony, believe dat," Abdullah ranted, disconnecting the cordless telephone.

Ebony froze in shock for a few minutes before she slammed down the receiver in its cradle in disgust.

The moment Ebony ended her relationship with Abdullah was the very moment feelings he had no idea he had for her crept up flooding his heart. It was at that very moment that Abdullah realized that he was also in love with Ebony.

"Abdullah! Abdullah! Snap out of it," Daniel barked playfully, flaunting a smile. "Are you okay?"

"I'm cool," Abdullah said calmly.

"Dude, that was some awesome stuff you had," Daniel proclaimed with wide eyes.

"I always got nothing but the best. Believe dat. I got ten onions of dat good shit for you. Dat goes to the payment for the BMW," Abdullah retorted, as he handed Daniel a bag that contained ten ounces of powder cocaine.

"Look here, dude! Look what I got for you," Daniel said excitedly, handing Abdullah a tiny chrome .22-caliber Derringer pistol.

Menacingly, displaying a monstrous facial expression, Abdullah leveled the handgun as if he were at target practice, as if he were gunning down an individual.

Daniel instantly grew wary by Abdullah's troubling demeanor.

"Now don't you go out there and hurt anybody," Daniel said with concern in his voice.

"Do I look like I would hurt somebody? Little ole me, I'm harmless, this is for protection," Abdullah replied, peering at the firearm he clutched.

*****

An emotional wreck, Ebony paced back and forth in her bedroom, as she eagerly fingered the numbers to the telephone she held.

Ring, ring, ring, ring, the telephone intoned.

"Hello?" Trish said softly.

"Trish, it's over. I finally quit Abdullah," Ebony announced.

"Don't worry about him, girl, it's going to be all right," Trish said sharply, pretending to comfort her best friend while she wore a sinister facial expression, lounging on a chair in her family room.

"He...he didn't even care, he could care less that I was ending our relationship," Ebony whined.

*****

"Now check this out," Daniel said boisterously as he waved a sawed-off shotgun.

"Fuck yeah! Let me get dat!" Abdullah roared.

"It's yours, my little friend. You take care of me, I take care of you," Daniel expounded.

*****

"Ebony, I need to use the phone," Ebony's mother informed while she reared her head in to her daughter's bedroom to discover Ebony's face soaked in tears.

"Trish, I'll call you back. My mom has to use the phone," Ebony relayed.

"All right, call me later. Bye," Trish fired back.

"Bye," Ebony said, disconnecting her telephone from her long-time best friend.

*****

Moments later, Ebony's mother strolled into her bedroom, smoothly dropping onto her bed, gazing square into her misty eyes.

"What's wrong? Why are you crying?" Ebony's mother asked in a warm, gentle voice as wiped her daughter's teary eyes with a tissue.

"Mom, I'm okay, I'm fine," Ebony said in unease, avoiding eye contact, looking away from her mother.

"Ebony, be clear with me. Something is wrong. Tell me, baby, what is it?" Ebony's mother said with a concerned facial expression.

"Fine, Mom, you win. Remember that boy that used to call all the time but suddenly stopped? Well?"

"You mean Abdullah?" Ebony's mother questioned, cutting her daughter off before she could finish what she was saying.

"Yes, Mom I mean Abdullah. We just broke up," Ebony confirmed with exhaustion in her voice.

"Why?" Ebony's mother replied.

"He sort of hurt me. He was missing in action for thirteen months, then out of the blue I run into him. His excuse for being absent all the time was he was incarcerated. The funny thing is he never revealed why or what he was in jail for! I really don't know if he's being honest, and I can't be with someone I can't trust. Something about him is fishy, but I love him so much," Ebony said weakly with despair, leaping from her voice as her mind flashed back to Pennsylvania with Abdullah behind the wheel of the BMW, clutching his lethal weapon.

"Trust is a major factor in a relationship. Without it, verily it will not last. I am trying to wrap my head around the fact that you were dealing with somebody who was in jail, a criminal. Red flags should be waving in your head, Ebony, Abdullah sounds like big trouble. Let him go, forget about him," Ebony's mother said candidly.

"But you see, Mom, Abdullah is not a criminal. He's lying about being in jail. He's just using that as an excuse on why he didn't keep in contact for months. He's a good person, he can't do no wrong. He's a law-abiding citizen," Ebony rationalized, contradicting herself, not being too truthful to her mother.

*****

Abdullah climbed back into the Beemer, tossing a key into the ignition, waking the engine. Just as Abdullah was about to pull off, Trish appeared in his head. Realizing that he hadn't called Trish, realizing that he needed to call her, Abdullah quickly cut the vehicle off, anxiously darting back to Daniel's front doorstep. After several knocks, Daniel appeared with his nose caked with powder cocaine.

"What's happening? Come on in," said an amped-up Daniel, ushering Abdullah back in his house.

"I need to use your horn again," Abdullah said hurriedly.

"Sure thing, little buddy," Daniel said, nonchalantly sniffling his street candy.

Steeping back into the plush living room, Abdullah swiftly grabbed the cordless telephone, finger-tapping the numbers while his heart violently bounced around in his chest.

The telephone rang three times before a sweet tiny voice leaped onto the line.

"Hello?"

"Hello? Is Trish there?" Abdullah replied.

"This is her, who is this?" Trish responded.

"Abdullah," he said calmly.

"Hey, I was waiting for you to call," Trish said warmly.

"I had to take care of some things. I talked to Ebony too, it's a wrap. It's over, me and her are history," Abdullah fired back.

"Yeah, I know. She told me. She said you didn't care. Abdullah, she's heartbroken. She was crying, she's really hurting right now," Trish said sorrowfully.

"Trish, I don't give a fuck about Ebony. You're all I care about and think about. You know what she said to me? Abdullah, I got to let you go. I said bye! It ain't bout nuffin, dat girl is wack," Abdullah said firmly.

"Honestly, Abdullah, when we were up in Pennsylvania, she was talking about quitting you. That was all she kept talking about. She says she loves you, but she says it's something about you that is not right," Trish divulged.

"Something about me isn't right? Trish, she's bugging, fuck dat bitch! I got you now, and I'm gonna tell her dat. I got you too, fuck dat," Abdullah said vividly.

"Are you for real? Are you really gonna tell her," Trish said dumbfounded.

Chapter 16

"What do you think, I'm bullshitting?" Abdullah said banteringly.

"No, no, no, I don't think you're bullshitting. But let's hold off on telling her about us," Trish replied softly.

"All right, dat's cool, we'll wait," Abdullah agreed.

"So when am I gonna see you again?" Trish queried.

"Whenever you want. Shiiiiiit, I'll come by later on if dat's what you want me to do," Abdullah retorted.

"That's exactly what I want you to do. Come by later on, eight o'clock would be nice. Okay?" Trish said gently.

"I'll be over there, word," Abdullah said confidently.

"I'll be waiting too! Bye," Trish said in a joyous tone.

"Bye," Abdullah followed.

They hung up.

*****

With NWA's "Always Into Somethin'" leaping voraciously from the car radio's speakers, Abdullah pulled up in front of Trish's residence. He peered at the watch that wrapped his wrist. The wristwatch read 7:57 p.m. Abdullah simply cut off the engine and closed his eyes, reclining behind the wheel of the '92 candy-apple red BMW 525i.

Minutes later, Abdullah opened his eyes calmly, checking the time one his watch, which displayed 8:03 p.m. Swiftly, Abdullah climbed out of the BMW, making his way to Trish's front doorstep.

"Exhaling deeply, Abdullah finger-tapped the doorbell. In a matter of minutes, the front door swung open, exhibiting a woman with a pale-golden complexion smiling through her narrow eyes.

"Hi, Abdullah, I am Miss Jongnam, Trish's mother. Nice to meet you," she said amiably.

"Hey, Miss Jongnam, nice to meet you too," Abdullah replied with a slight smile.

"Come on in," Trish's mother said invitingly.

Abdullah stepped into the dwelling, tailing the lady—that Trish resembled—through the house, ultimately landing in the entertainment room.

"Make yourself at home," Miss Jongnam said in a hospitable tone as she gestured with her head for Abdullah to have a seat, who flopped on to the near sofa. "Would you like to have something to drink? We have iced tea, Kool-Aid, soda, and ice water.

"Yes, Miss Jongnam I would like to have some iced tea," Abdullah said politely.

Moments later, Trish breezed into the entertainment room. "I am sorry I took so long. I was putting the finishing touches on our dinner. I made us spaghetti, my specialty," Trish proclaimed with confidence escaping from her voice, as she motioned toward the dining room.

The twosome strode into the dining room, encountering a table that was elegantly decorated with candles, napkins, silverware. There was a pitcher filled with iced tea accompanied with two tall glasses that also held iced tea. There were two plates piled with spaghetti, along with slices of garlic bread. And with that, smiling ear to ear, Abdullah promptly took control of the situation, pulling out a chair for the girl he was head over heels for. Trish settled into her seat, and Abdullah followed suit.

"You is something else," Abdullah marveled, peering deep into the windows of Trish's eyes.

"I hope you enjoy my spaghetti, I really do. You should know that I want to make you happy. Did I make you happy tonight?" Trish said softly.

"Hell yeah, you made me happy. I'm happy just to be in your presence, you just don't know," Abdullah said exultantly.

"I mean I have never—and I mean never—cooked for any boy in my life…before," Trish said singleheartedly.

"I'm not just any bol, I'm a bol who loves you to death," Abdullah contended.

Uncontrollably, Trish beamed at Abdullah's response.

Moments later while the pair quietly downed their spaghetti, they intensely observed one another. Trish reached over the table, taking Abdullah's hand into hers. Then she broke the silence that dwelled in between the two.

"Abdullah, make me a promise," Trish said firmly.

"All right, what's the promise?" Abdullah said eagerly as he noticed the sudden change in Trish's demeanor from delightful to sorrowful.

"Promise me that you will never ever leave me, that you will always be here for me, no matter what the circumstances are. Promise me, Abdullah," Trish said earnestly.

"Baby, I ain't going nowhere, believe dat. I promise you I'm here. I don't care what the circumstances are. Now you promise me dat you will always be in my life, dat you'll be my wife, and someday you'll have my baby. Promise me," Abdullah replied.

Trish flashed a smile. "I promise you, Abdullah, I will always be in your life. I promise I will be your wife, and in the future when we are much older, I promise I will give you a baby."

"This is our promise, we can't break it by any means," Abdullah said with conviction.

"Our promise, our cardinal rule," Trish fired back.

Shortly after the twosome finished their dinner, Trish eased up out of her seat. She gestured with her finger, letting Abdullah know to hold on. Then she proceeded into the entertainment room.

Trish made her way to the stereo, frantically shuffling through the tapes that sat in a cubicle on the side of the sound system. In a matter of seconds, Trish came across what she was searching for, grasping the cassette. Gently, Trish inserted the tape into the tape deck. Instantly, "Always" by Pebbles flowed from the stereo speakers.

Trish bolted back to the dining room where Abdullah sat patiently. She summoned him with her finger, wiggling her lone finger.

Without any hesitation, Abdullah sprang to his feet, trailing Trish back to the entertainment room.

"Do you wanna dance?" Trish said smoothly, grabbing Abdullah by the hand, pulling him close to her body.

Abdullah nodded yes, fitting his hands around Trish's waistline, shifting her to the melody of pebbles. The teenage couple examined the windows of each other's eyes as their lips slowly connected.

Animatedly, Abdullah kissed Trish's lips, while she kissed his lips. Then he savagely sucked her bottom lip, then her top lip. Promptly, the young lovers ceased lip locking, passionately gazing at one another for a minute before they continued their lip-and-tongue game.

Miss Jongnam appeared in the doorway of the entertainment room, causing Abdullah to flinch, breaking away from Trish as if he didn't just have his tongue down her throat.

Miss Jongnam snickered at Abdullah's vain attempt to act as if he weren't just kissing her daughter. Subsequently, Miss Jongnam gestured to Trish that she had a call, holding her hand shaped as if it was a telephone to her ear.

*****

"Hello?" Trish sang into the receiver, now sitting in the living room.

"What are you doing?" Ebony inquired.

"Nothing, girl, I was just listening to the radio, bored as hell," Trish slowly answered.

"I'm bored too. There's nothing really on TV. I wonder what that damn Abdullah is doing right now. You know what, he didn't even call back to try to make up. I should page him," Ebony replied.

"Are you gonna make up with him?" Trish asked, concealing the dread that invaded her mind.

"I do not even know. I don't know what it is about that boy, but I cannot get him out of my head. It's like I cannot live with him, but at the same time I cannot live without him. I'm gonna page him as soon as I hang up with you. I really need to talk to him," Ebony said earnestly.

"You're not wrong, you're right. Call him, do not let him go. Don't you dare. I don't know why you ended it in the first place. Ebony, you love Abdullah. I hate to see my best friend hurting, so when you hang up with me, you page him and you tell him how much he means to you," Trish chided.

"Where is this coming from? What's wrong with you? Why do you sound so angry?" Ebony queried, her voice filled with bafflement.

"I sound like this because I am angry you have an opportunity to be with the person you love, and you're taking that for granted. Look at me, just look at me. Jax is dead and gone. I don't have the luxury to be with the person I love anymore. Look, all I'm saying is that you truly love Abdullah, so don't take that for granted. Don't waste your time. Life is short, don't let him go," Trish said emotionally.

Ebony sighed. "You're right, girl. I'll call you tomorrow, okay?" she said.

"Bye," Trish said plainly.

"Bye," Ebony fired back.

Click! The best friends hung up.

Meanwhile, Abdullah sat in a chair that sat on the side of the stereo. While Sade's "Nothing Can Come Between Us" danced from the speaker. A smiling Ebony flashed in his mind. Abdullah couldn't elude the feelings he held deep inside for Ebony. But he could act, and that's exactly what he did.

Returning to the entertainment room, Trish discovered Abdullah reading the screen of his pager.

"It's Ebony, right?" Trish said dryly.

"Yeah, how you know?" Abdullah replied with raised eyebrows.

"I just got done talking to her," Trish informed.

"What was she talking about?" Abdullah pried.

Trish sighed. "She wants you back. It hasn't been a whole day yet, and she wants to talk to you. She can't let go."

"This is crazy," Abdullah said hurriedly.

"You can't call her," Trish said abruptly and excitedly. "I mean, you can't call her from here. We can't let her know about us, not yet anyway."

"Don't worry, she won't find out about us until you're ready to tell her," Abdullah assured, rising out of his chair to embrace Trish. Trish escorted Abdullah to the living room where they settled onto a couch in front of the television.

"I have something I need to tell you," Trish said gently.

"What is it?" Abdullah said anxiously.

"I am still a virgin," Trish divulged.

"Yeah? You and Jax didn't do it?" Abdullah fired back, acting as if he were clueless.

"We were about to the night Jax was murdered," Trish replied, as she dropped her head. "I wonder if they're ever gonna catch Jax's murderer. It's going on two years, and the cops still haven't found the killer. Do you think the killer got away?"

"I don't know, but it's been a minute. They say the longer a murder goes unsolved, the harder it is to solve. We might not never know who killed Jax," Abdullah role played.

"Ab, sometimes I wonder if my dad and Jax are together in heaven. Do you think they're watching us now?" Trish said in a child-like tone, flashing a weak smile, locking eyes with Abdullah.

"They might be, Trish. When did your dad die?" Abdullah acted with a hint of concern in his voice.

"Nine months ago in a car accident. Are you afraid to die? I am. I don't want to die, Abdullah. I fear death, I really do. I lost Jax, lost my dad. I can't lose you too. I can't. Please stay alive, please," Trish said grievously.

"I'm not afraid to die. I ain't gonna die, not yet. I'ma live to be an old man," Abdullah crowed.

Chapter 17

The following rainy night in Kennett Square, Pennsylvania, in a lusterless and shabby alley parking lot, Abdullah slouched in the passenger seat of Kuba's parked '79 white Lincoln continental town coupe ear-soaking the earsplitting cut of "Nuthin' But a G Thang" by Dr. Dre and Snoop Dogg, while his brother stood near in the clashing rain on a pay telephone.

"He's not here yet. He should be pulling up in any minute. You gave me your word dat you wouldn't kill him, Kuba," the lady on the line said firmly.

"Relax a little, you said you didn't care about the bol. Remember you ain't got no real feelings for him, it's just about his dough. Now you crying, talking 'bout you gave me your word shit. Fuck dat nut ass, nigga. Everything is going down as I planned, all right?" Kuba replied sharply.

"Alright baby, I'll put 911 in your beeper when Brian comes back," the lady on the telephone said submissively.

"Yo, it's raining like cats and dogs out this bitch. I'm getting ready to sit in my ride. Just page me when dat nigga comes back," Kuba expounded.

"Kuba, do you still love me? Do you think we'll ever get back together again?" the lady questioned.

"Denise, why you trying to get all lovey-dovey with me?" Kuba said hurriedly.

"'Cuz I miss you," Denise retorted.

"You miss me? Why you ain't never come see me when I was in a cage?" Kuba fired back with skepticism in his voice.

"I didn't," Denise paused, then she continued. "Want to see you all locked up? Dat would have hurt me to see you down on your luck.

But now dat you're home, I'm gonna make up for the time I was out of your life for everything."

"Then act like you know what time it is. Stop crying 'bout dat nut-ass motherfucker," Kuba scoffed.

"You know, I got a baby by the guy. He's my daughter's dad, you know?" Denise said compassionately.

"Yeah, and dat's the only reason why I ain't gonna smoke dat nigga. I'm just gonna take his birds," Kuba said sternly.

"Hold on, I think dat's him," Denise said animatedly as she placed the receiver down to see if her baby's father was pulling up. "No it ain't him, but I'll call you back, all right? Bye. Oh remember 911."

Kuba eased behind the wheel of his vehicle, reaching over to the car radio, turning down Dr. Dre's "The Chronic" at a low tone.

"As soon as the broad beeps me, we're out," Kuba said plainly, glancing at his brother, then peering into the deluge out of the dimmed alley across the hilly two-way street that was furnished with raggedy congested homes.

"Yo I don't know what's up with Reishee, he was supposed to meet me up West Chester, but he didn't show. I hope he didn't get bagged," Abdullah said warily.

"Where the loot and coke at from y'all caper?" Kuba queried.

"I got thirteen geez from the caper, but Reishee got the coke. We didn't divide it up yet. I think something happened, though, 'cuz he wouldn't rob me," Abdullah replied.

"Damn, you don't know what happen, do you?" Kuba said soberly with saddened eyes.

"What you mean? What happened?" Abdullah asked in confusion.

"You must haven't been watching the TV. Reishee and Gwen was all over the news. The police was chasing them in Philly. They got trapped in a roadblock on the Ben Franklin. They said they jumped from the bridge," Kuba said sincerely.

Violently, in a fit of rage, Abdullah pounded his fist against the dashboard while his eyes watered from the discouraging and heart-breaking news.

"You think he made it? You think they made it?" Abdullah said as his voice shook with emotion.

"Nah, Ab, I don't see them surviving. In the news they said they had a search team trying to recover the bodies. And when they say dat, it's pretty much all she wrote. They're gone," Kuba said quietly and candidly, peering out of the windshield as the rain fiercely spanked against it.

With dread consuming his being, Abdullah hung his head. "Reishee and Gwen wanted to die instead of going to jail," he said in a soft tone with a hint of bewilderment before raising his head, planting his eyes on his brother, who still gazed out of the windshield.

"Some people would rather die than spend the rest of their life in the bing. Reishee and Gwen were deep in them streets. They have a whole lot of jawns, I mean bodies! I can't say dat if was in their shoes. I would've done the same thing I can't say, life in a cage... I'd rather die in the streets free," Kuba said earnestly, still looking straight ahead.

Abdullah sighed. "Has a chick ever cooked for you before?" he said naively, varying from the subject, switching to a lighter mood.

"Yeah," Kuba said calmly, accompanied with a chuckled.

"Last night a girl cooked for me," Abdullah divulged in a hypnotize state.

"What she cook?" Kuba pried as amusement masked his face.

"Spaghetti," Abdullah uttered.

"What?" Kuba fired back.

"Spaghetti," Abdullah repeated.

"All man, you didn't eat spaghetti, noooooo," Kuba japed, smiling.

"You act like I did something wrong or something," Abdullah said with a clueless facial expression.

"Ab, dat girl might have been on her period. Dat's a trick. When broads be bleeding, they doctor up their spaghetti with their blood to hook a nigga," Kuba said as he laughed uncontrollably.

"She didn't have to put her blood in my spaghetti, 'cuz I'm already hooked, believe dat. She got her hooks all in me," Abdullah fired back.

122

"The chocolate jawn you was with the other night?" Kuba queried.

"Nah, her girl. The half Asian and black jawn," Abdullah relayed as he smiled ear to ear.

Beaming, Kuba nodded in approval. "They both bad though," he chirped referencing Ebony's and Trish's pleasing features.

Kuba's pager tingled in his pocket. Anxiously, Kuba extracted the loot clocker, scanning the face that displayed 911.

Reading his brother's body language, Abdullah stepped out of the Lincoln, encountering the pouring rain, with Kuba following suit.

"Mommom wants you to come by the house. She wants us to eat together as a family, you know? So after this, let's go by there," Abdullah said sincerely as he walked side by side with his brother through the blistering rain.

"All right, we'll go over there after we handle this," Kuba replied.

*****

Meanwhile, from across the street on the opposite side of the shabby alley where the brothers toed through, Denise energetically paced back and forth in her worn-down home.

Quickly, the brothers crossed the two-way street through the thin traffic, ultimately ending up in front of Denise's stoop. In a sudden instant, three hooded figures emerged from out of the night, opening fire on Abdullah and Kuba with their assault rifles as they raced toward the siblings from the opposite directions, two from the top of the street and one from the bottom of street.

"Abdullah, get down," Kuba said urgently, pushing his brother behind one of the parked cars that lined the hilly two-way street, while he drew his firearm, returning fire on the mysterious gunmen.

Spraying up the street wildly, the sole gunman from the lowest part of the block carelessly made his way up the street as if he was invincible. Through the chaos of gun play, Abdullah erected his pistol from the car he hid behind, aggressively unleashing slugs into the lone gunman who moved from the lower part of the street.

The triggerman tumbled onto the wet pavement, as his blood mingled with the rain, swarming into the gutter.

Swiftly, Abdullah spun around to discover his brother plastered against a parked car headlight, consumed with agony, wounded with bullets to his abdomen and shoulders.

Standing straight up, Abdullah feverishly rushed to Kuba while leveling his firearm in the direction of the hooded figures, letting the lead fly. Cautiously, the hooded donned men took cover behind the parked cars that decorated the hill-shaped street.

"What the fuck did I get us into? Dat dirty bitch set us up!" Kuba said regretfully, sitting in the wet street with Abdullah, kneeling next to him, sandwiched in between two cars out of the hooded figures' trajectory who repeatedly pumped slugs through the automobile bodies, knocking out their windows.

Unprepared and outgunned for war, Abdullah and Kuba's pistols were no match by far for the AK-47s the disguised men clutched.

"I only got one clip. In a minute I'll be out," Abdullah said warily.

"I got two. Before we know it, I'll be down to one. We gotta hit these cats," Kuba said in a feeble tone, gathering his strength and arising to his feet animatedly, dumping his .44 semiautomatic on their adversaries.

Subsequently, Abdullah assisted his brother, unloading his four-pound on the hooded figures.

While the rain violently showered from the heavens, the brothers exchanged bullets with the cloaked figures, back and forth, back and forth, back and forth as they ducked and dodged behind the parked cars.

Upon emptying their lethal weapons, Abdullah and Kuba reverted back in between the parked cars.

"My fault, Ab, I didn't mean to get you all caught up in this shit. Take heed, learn from this, you hear me? If a motherfucker should ever betray you, I don't give a fuck how small it is. I don't give a fuck what it's about, you cut them off. The small things always turn in big things. Don't give them a chance to back stab you. Don't... I love you, Ab," Kuba said sincerely, as his voice quivered from the pain the slugs waged, slipping the remaining cartridge into his firearm.

Kuba sighed. "Listen, it ain't no need for both of us to die tonight, so here's what's going down. I'm gonna run straight at them niggaz, going for dome shots. When I'm doing dat you're gonna roll, you're gonna jet," he said with saddened, dreadful, moistened eyes.

"I can't leave you, I can't! We just gotta die together," Abdullah exclaimed as disbelief and sadness grasped his being while the rain relentlessly dropped from the sky.

"No... No! No! Abdullah, tell mommom and poppop I love them," Kuba said firmly.

Then Kuba bolted toward the hooded figures as if he had a death wish, firing upon them with Abdullah looking on. Prepared for the attack, the cloaked gunmen had the drop on Kuba, leveling their assault rifles, riddling his chest with lead, causing Abdullah's eyes to widen in shock and terror.

Kuba buckled, landing back first onto the wet sidewalk, while Abdullah peeked from the rear of a parked car.

Immediately, the hooded figures fled into the rainy night as the sirens from the ambulance and police vehicles filled the air from an unknown distance, gradually drawing near.

Frantically, Abdullah made his way to his brother who lay twisted on the wet pavement. Abdullah took the barely alive Kuba into his arms while a fleet of police cruisers and ambulances raced to the ghastly crime scene.

"I'm dying, it's all she wrote for me. Get away from here. I love you!! Gooooo... La ilaha illa, Allah, Muhammadur asoolu, Allah," Kuba said weakly, before he shook and died.

A lone tear trickled down Abdullah's face as he placed his brother onto the wet concrete. Briskly, Abdullah dug into Kuba's pockets removing his pager, car keys, and a large knot of dead presidents.

Abdullah darted across the hilly two-way street, zigzagging through traffic eventually, sliding behind the wheel of the '79 white Lincoln Continental Town Coupe, pulling off.

Eager to elude the authorities, Abdullah torpedoed through the streets of Kennett Square through the vibrant rainfall. Two blocks away, discovering red and blue flashing lights along with roaring sirens, Abdullah eased his foot from the accelerator. In a matter of minutes, a team of squad cars and ambulances zoomed pass Abdullah.

*****

The next day, on a radiant afternoon in Camden, New Jersey, Abdullah cruised through a residential neighborhood. Street after street after street, he inspected the vehicles that furnished the roads. After prowling numerous blocks, Abdullah finally came upon what he was searching for, a white Lincoln, identical to the one he wheeled. Meticulously, Abdullah circled the block, making sure that there were no badges around, lurking. Now a block away from the white Lincoln that Abdullah discovered, he parked and hopped out of the vehicle with a screwdriver in hand.

Standing at the rear of the white Lincoln, Abdullah artfully and smoothly unscrewed the license plate. Then he quickly reverted to Kuba's Lincoln, speeding off into the sunshine.

*****

Mays Landing, New Jersey
In a room that was adorned with extravagant furniture with walls that were overlapping with mirrors corner to corner, Abdullah sat, comfortably accompanied by a sandy-complexioned teenage girl who possessed enticing features. The sounds of En Vogue flooded the room.

"Ab, where you been? You ain't been in Jersey in a while," the sandy-complexioned teenage girl said exuberantly, smiling brightly.

"Jessica, I was locked up in the youth study center. I just got out the other day. What's up? I'm here now, though," Abdullah replied.

"Oh you here now… I can see dat," Jessica smart-mouthed as she looked Abdullah up and down, climbing out of her seat, sliding out of the room, toeing up the stairs.

Without uttering a single word Abdullah traced Jessica's foot-steps, ultimate coming face-to-face with her in her bedroom.

Jessica flopped onto the bed, spreading her legs, with the look of seduction in her eyes. Subsequently, Abdullah followed suit, crawling over Jessica's petite figure, embracing her. Their tongues wrestled.

*****

Meanwhile in Claymont, Delaware, in Ebony's house, the telephone roared. Calmly, she made her way to the telephone and scooped it from the table.

"Hello?" Ebony sang into the receiver.

"Hey, Ebony, what chu doing?" Trish said amiably.

"Nothing. You know I was just about to call you too. Abdullah hasn't called me back since I paged him," Ebony said dryly.

"Are you serious?" Trish replied.

Wow, I haven't heard from him either, Trish thought to herself.

"Trish, last night I couldn't sleep. I just kept thinking about Abdullah, but I'm not gonna sweat him. He knows my number," Ebony said with denial leaping from her voice.

"Forget about Abdullah, don't worry about him. You do not need to be losing sleep over his punk ass," Trish said bluntly.

Ironically, Trish was in the same boat as her best friend. She too couldn't sleep the night before. She couldn't get Abdullah out of her mind.

"A few days ago, you said that I should try to get back with Abdullah if I really loved him. And now you're saying forget him," Ebony said in confusion.

"That's right, I said that. Look, you're my best friend. I hate to see you hurting. Abdullah not calling is the crap he pulled before. I am not telling you to completely forget him, but if he does not call, come on, Ebony. You can't keep beating a dead horse," Trish retorted.

"I'm not letting go. I love Abdullah," Ebony said firmly.

*****

As Jessica held open the doors to her love tunnel, Abdullah glided his manhood into her wetness.

Poking the insides of her warmth, her love box grew wetter and wetter. "Fuck me, Ab. Fuck me. Oooooooh, fuck me," Jessica howled in pleasure as Abdullah vigorously beat her kitty cat.

Within a matter of minutes, their bodies were erupting and quivering in sheer ecstasy.

Chapter 18

In the nightfall of Kennett Square, Pennsylvania, decked out in a woman's wig and dress and cleverly disguised as a female, Abdullah stepped to Denise's front door. Calmly, he tapped on the front door. Minutes later, the front door swung open, revealing a man in his early thirties along with KRS-One's "Black Cop," which blared from the rear of the house. Unwittingly, the man bought Abdullah's disguise, due to his baby-faced appearance and small stature.

"Is Denise here?" Abdullah asked in a girlish voice.

"No, she just went to the store," the man replied.

"Do you know who I am?" Abdullah queried softly.

"Nah, who are you?" the man questioned, holding a dull facial expression.

"I'm the grim reaper!" Abdullah roared with flaming eyes as he produced a small chrome .22-caliber Derringer pistol, leveling it point-blank to the man's chest.

Pop! Pop! the bullets tore through the man's heart. He collapsed in the doorway of the home.

Nonchalantly, Abdullah stepped over the barely alive man, whose life was fading away quickly. Proceeding into the residence, Abdullah threw the small firearm to the floor. Subsequently, whipping out a sawed-off shotgun, following the trail of the knocking "Black Cop Beat," Abdullah carefully inched through the home, brandishing the deadly weapon.

Abdullah peered into a room to find Denice's baby's dad bopping around as if he were on the soul train accompanied by a man resembling him, who could be his brother and who sat in a chair, tossing his head back and forth.

Without any hesitation and with no mercy in the windows of his eyes, Abdullah aimed his lethal weapon at Denice's baby's dad. The shotgun blast struck him in the face, decapitating him, flinging his blood, brains, and parts of his face and head against the wall.

Fazed by what he had just witnessed, the man in the chair held his hands in the air in submission.

"Hold up. Let's talk, man, let's talk! Please! Let's talk about this!" the man screamed in vain as the booming music drowned his rants with horror possessing him.

Abdullah approached his brother's killer and unloaded the shotgun shells into his chest.

*****

Abdullah pulled up into an isolated area that equipped a dumpster. He quickly departed the vehicle and shot to the rear of the Lincoln. Swiftly, with a screwdriver in hand, Abdullah unscrewed the New Jersey license plate, removing the plate from the vehicle, replacing it with a real Pennsylvania tag. Abdullah reverted to the driver's side, leaning inside the automobile, pulling out a bag.

With a lot of motivation, Abdullah stripped out of the female attire, throwing the clothes into the bag. He ripped off the woman's wig, dropping it into the bag. Then he pelted off his gloves, tossing them into the bag. He strolled to the dumpster, disposing the evidence that the authorities would love to have.

Hours later in the darkness of Claymont, Delaware, Abdullah maneuvered the 92 candy-apple red BMW 525i in front of a 7-Eleven that lined Philadelphia Pike. He climbed out of the Beemer and made his way to the telephone booth, slamming twenty-five cents into the talk machine, finger-tapping the numbers. Nine rings passed before someone answered.

"Hello?" a lady with a light foreign accent sang into the receiver.

"Hi! How you doing, Miss Jongnam?" Abdullah greeted.

"Fine and you?" Miss Jongnam replied.

"I'm fine, is Trish there?" Abdullah said politely.

"Yes, but I'm on the phone. I'll tell her you called, call her back. Bye," Miss Jongnam said comfortably.

"Bye," Abdullah fired back.

Click! They hung up.

Ring, ring, ring, ring, ring, ring, the telephone intoned.

"Hello?" Ebony sang calmly into the telephone.

"Hello?" Abdullah followed.

"Abdullah? Well, it's about time you called," Ebony smart-mouthed.

"Kuba's dead," Abdullah announced in a disheartening voice.

"What? Oh my goodness, what happened?" Ebony exclaimed in shock.

"Can I see you? Ebony, I need to see you for real," Abdullah said in urgency.

"You can see me? Of course you can, I'm babysitting tonight, okay?" Ebony said softly.

*****

In a pitch-black room lounged Abdullah and Ebony, watching the television that provided the only light, while the kids that Ebony babysat snugged in their beds.

Abdullah eased his hands onto Ebony's thighs and artfully caressed them. Then he fingered his way down her legs, ending up at her love box. He palmed and massaged her kitty cat as she squirmed from his tender touch. Feverishly, he unfastened her pants. Stopping him in his tracks, she layered her hands over his, gesturing for him to quit.

"What's wrong?" Abdullah asked with a puzzled facial expression.

Ebony sighed. "I don't feel like it," she proclaimed dully.

"Why not?" Abdullah questioned as he held a look on his face that read, "You got to be kidding me."

"Because, Abdullah, I just don't feel like doing it," Ebony answered.

"Ebony, why you acting like dat?" Abdullah fired back.

Abdullah's pager erupted. Quickly, he snatched the loot clocker from his hip, inspecting the numbers that appeared in the screen. As soon as he realized that Trish was tagging him, he smiled slyly.

Unexpectedly, Ebony grabbed Abdullah's pager.

"Stop playing! Give me my pager back," Abdullah said sternly, in a panic.

"No! Why was you smiling? Who's paging you?" Ebony pried with irritation leaping from her voice.

Abdullah grew tense, out of fear that Ebony would discover that her best friend was paging him.

"My brother just got killed, and you're worried about who's paging me? Come on, man," Abdullah said pointedly, placing the guilt trip on Ebony.

Ebony dropped her head. "You're right, Ab. I'm sorry," she said gently, handing Abdullah his loot clocker.

"I'm out!" Abdullah ranted, storming to the front door, stepping out of the house.

"Abdullah! Abdullah! Come back," Ebony cried out, standing still.

By the time Ebony made it to the doorway, Abdullah was pulling off. Angered by Abdullah's haste departure, Ebony thrust her fist against the wall.

Moments later, Abdullah returned to the 7-Eleven, slinging a quarter into the pay telephone.

"Hello?" Trish's mother answered.

"Hello? Miss Jongnam? Can I speak to Trish?" Abdullah said in a pleasant tone.

"Yes, hold on," Miss Jongnam replied.

"Hey, Abdullah," Trish said warmly.

"What's going on?" Abdullah fired back.

"I am sitting here watching Def Comedy Jam, where are you?" Trish said in harmony.

"I'm at the 7-Eleven, the one down the road from you," Abdullah informed.

"What you doing out this way?" Trish queried.

"I just was with Ebony when you paged me. She snatched my beeper..."

Trish cut Abdullah off before he could finish what he was saying. "Does she know I paged you?" she asked in suspense.

"Nah, she don't know," Abdullah said, then he sighed. "Kuba's dead, he got killed."

"Aw, Abdullah, are you okay? If you want to talk about it, we can. Don't be afraid, I am here for you," Trish said sincerely.

"I'm cool, Trish, when can we talk in person?" Abdullah said calmly.

"Tomorrow if you like," Trish replied. "My mom goes to work at eight in the morning, so be over by nine."

"I'll be there," Abdullah said confidently, as he smiled ear to ear.

"You better," Trish fired back, chuckling.

"Are you gonna cook for me again?" Abdullah inquired.

"Yes indeed, Ab, I want to please you. I want to make you happy. I know you're in a lot of pain right now, I was there. I know exactly how you feel," Trish said as she got sentimental.

Chapter 19

The following morning, Trish stood in her kitchen gracefully and artfully cracking an egg's shell, spilling its yolk into the skillet, she hovered over while Patti Labelle's, "The Best Is Yet To Come" played throughout the house.

Filled with excitement, Trish got ready to see the love of her life. She couldn't wait to rest in Abdullah's arms; she couldn't wait to gaze into his eyes.

*****

With "Ghetto Bastard" by Naughty By Nature blaring out of the BMW's speakers, Abdullah pulled up in front of Trish's house, only to find her in the window of her bedroom, smiling broadly.

Swiftly, Trish left the window, rushing into the bathroom. Now standing in front of the mirror, Trish animatedly examined herself, making sure that there wasn't any sleep lodged in the corner of her eyes, licking her lips and fluffing her hair. Then she breezed out of the lavatory.

Frantically, from the kitchen to the dining room, Trish transported her and Abdullah's plates that were decorated with scrambled eggs, turkey sausages, and toast accompanied with jelly and butter.

Repeatedly, the doorbell rang out in harmony.

"I'll be right there!" Trish shouted as she hustled to the front door.

Fluffing her hair one last time, Trish swung the door open to discover Abdullah holding a "serious as twenty-five to life" facial expression.

"Hey, Ab," Trish said happily, while her eyes lit up.

"What's up, Trish?" Abdullah replied, stepping into her residence.

Abdullah tailed Trish into the dining room.

"See what I made you, baby?" Trish said affectionately, holding her arms in the air, standing near the dining table.

"You is something else, I'll tell you," Abdullah commented with a smile.

"I'ma go get us some OJ," Trish declared.

Abdullah settled into a seat at the table while Trish left the dining room.

Moments later, Trish returned to the dining room where Abdullah ate greedily.

"So is it good?" Trish asked, flashing a smile, falling into a chair at the table and clutching two glasses of orange juice, sliding one across the table to Abdullah.

With a mouthful of Trish's cooking Abdullah replied with a nod. The adolescents sat in absolute silence, eyeing one another in between bites, beaming and gloating at one another in between bites. Many scoops and swigs were made before the young lovers' meal was completed. And with that, Trish led Abdullah into the living room. The teenage couple settled onto a couch.

With moving depressing eyes, Abdullah took a deep breath and turned to face Trish. "I've been down this street before. When I was seven my mom died right in front of me." He paused as he searched her eyes. "Dat's why you never heard me talk about her 'cuz she's gone. Now you know why I stay with mommom in Pennsylvania."

"Where's your dad?" Trish pried, displaying a sympathetic facial expression.

"He's gone too. He died before I was born," Abdullah informed. "My brother is dead... I still got my grandparents and an Auntie in Delaware. Dat's my gateway to this state. I held my brother just like you held Jax. He knew he was dying. He knew he was gonna die. He got shot up bad. I mean, blood was just pouring everywhere. This girl did Kuba dirty. He went to jail 'cuz of the bitch, got killed 'cuz of her. He loved her too, all man, did he. She wasn't right, though. She wasn't loyal. One day my brother was chilling with her at her crib. Her side thing came over with his crew. The nigga was packing, he pulled his heater, and Kuba grabbed it. The gun went off, killing the bol. By the time the trial rolled around, she cut my brother off, she had no rap. She left him hanging. Kuba was just trying to defend himself. He didn't mean to kill the bol, She didn't want to testify dat it was self-defense or nothing. You know what Kuba told me?" he said in anguish.

"It's going to be all right, baby, what did Kuba tell you?" Trish said softly as she seized Abdullah's hand.

"He said he love me, and he told me to tell our grandparents dat he loved them. Remember when we was up mommom's. She wanted to see Kuba, I told him. I told him, he didn't see death around the corner, until it was in his face," Abdullah said sorrowfully.

Trish leaned over and planted a juicy kiss on Abdullah's lips. Then she slowly leaned backward to observe his reaction.

"Damn, I love you," Abdullah proclaimed as he eased close to Trish, throwing his tongue down her throat.

Vigorously, the teenagers lip-locked as Abdullah climbed on top of Trish, while she lay back first on the couch.

Abdullah ran his hands up Trish's stomach, cupping a handful of her melons. Interfering with their game of foreplay, Trish sat up from the couch.

"Ab, let's do it. I want you," Trish panted.

With the quickness, the young lovers stripped.

Slowly, Abdullah inserted his manhood into Trish's love tunnel. Literally, he unleashed his seeds within a few beastie pumps. Blood gushed from out of Trish's walls. Abdullah rose up and sat on the couch. As he commenced to put on his boxers, Trish followed suit, throwing her panties on. Trish was in pain after the smashing of her cherry, even though she pretended not to be—her facial expression and body language spoke for itself.

Upon narrowing his gaze on Trish, Abdullah couldn't help but grin. *Trish, stop frontin'. You know I beat dat thang up. You'll never forget me*, he thought to himself.

"So was it how you expected it to be?" Trish asked naively.

"Yeah, your pussy was tighter than a motherfucker," Abdullah teased.

"Abdullah, of course my pussy was tight, I was a virgin. You took my virginity," Trish retorted as she punched Abdullah in his arm in a playful manner.

Abdullah and Trish sexed on and off until 5:00 p.m. Moments later, as Abdullah shuttled down Philadelphia Pike, his mind flashed to all the faces Trish made while he was penetrating her warmth.

Abdullah shifted the '92 candy-apple red BMW 525i into a Wawa parking lot, pulling up in front of the telephone booths that furnished the side of the establishment. He climbed out of the vehicle and made his way to the talk machine, drumming the eight hundred number to his pager.

"You have three messages," the voice mail sang.

"Abdullah, it's me, Ebony. Come over. I am home alone, bye."

"Yo! Ab, if you're still out Claymont, check me out. I'm at the top of the hill. I left Harbor House a while ago!"

"Hi, Abdullah, it's Trish. I know you just left, but I just wanted to say I love you."

Abdullah smiled ear to ear to the utterance of Trish's proclamation. Disconnecting his voice mail, Abdullah slammed a quarter into the talk machine, finger-tapping the number to the pay phone.

After three rings a murky voice invaded the line.

"Yo!" the murky-voiced man spat.

"Where Vernon at?" Abdullah inquired.

"Hold on," said the man with the murky voice.

"Ab, I need a double up," Vernon related.

"All right, I'm on my way, here I come," Abdullah said hurriedly, placing the receiver back onto its hook.

Chapter 20

Abdullah stepped into the apartment building off the top of the hill to find Vernon sitting quietly on the steps.

"What's up, Ab?" Vernon said as he flashed a smile.

"Money," Abdullah replied calmly, smiling.

Swiftly, the pair made the trade, exchanging dead presidents for street candy.

*****

Shortly thereafter, Abdullah toed up to Ebony's front door. He tapped on the front door a handful of times. No one answered so he knocked again, again, and again. Still not a peep from Ebony.

"Where the hell is this bitch at? Damn, I should have come straight here," Abdullah uttered to himself with a bit of regret while he commenced to bang on the front door animatedly.

Hesitatingly, Abdullah backed away from Ebony's front door, turning on his heels, and strolling toward the BMW. Just as Abdullah was about to fall behind the wheel of the vehicle, a familiar voice filled the air. "Abdullah! Abdullah!"

Abdullah spun around to discover Ebony standing in the doorway of her house, draped in a T-shirt and panties. Abdullah shut the door to the Beemer and made his way back to Ebony's house, as she vanished from the doorway.

Eagerly, Abdullah entered the residence to find Ebony seductively rubbing her titties, licking her lips, flinging her tongue up and down, gliding her hands down to her kitty cat, caressing it.

Instantly, Abdullah's manhood rocked up. Ebony gestured for Abdullah to follow her as she darted to her bedroom. Once they were situated in the bedroom, Ebony dropped to her knees and excitedly peeled off Abdullah's shorts. Then she quickly and savagely clutched his Johnson, placing him into her watery mouth.

Wide-eyed, Abdullah intently observed Ebony devouring his manhood. *Look at this silly-ass bitch here. If she only knew dat she's eating her own girl's pussy, silly-ass bitch*, he thought to himself, as he enjoyed the slob job, slightly smiling with a cunning facial expression.

"Hold up," Abdullah whispered in delight, withdrawing from the grasp of Ebony's jaws, flopping onto the bed, back first.

Like a furious tiger, Ebony crawled onto the bed over Abdullah, inserting him back into her watery mouth. Promptly, she sucked and licked violently. After giving Abdullah brain, Ebony squatted down onto his manhood while she held it in place. She bounced up and down as she gradually picked up the speed.

"Oh, oh, ooh, ooh, ooh, oooooooooh. Abdullah, it feels so good, baby. It feels so, so good," Ebony sang gratifyingly.

Abdullah palmed Ebony's rear cheeks, squeezing them together as she drove her warmness and wetness over his Johnson.

Passionately, their eyes connected while their bodies reached rapture.

"Do you love me?" Ebony muffled into Abdullah's ear as she held him tight.

Abdullah simply replied with a nod.

Immediately, Ebony broke their embrace and sprang up, peering directly into Abdullah's eyes as if she was seeking to read his mind.

"Do you?" Ebony asked again with a bit of skepticism in her voice, eyeing Abdullah keenly, waiting for an answer.

"Ebony, I love you," Abdullah fired back without blinking.

Chapter 21

Several months later, in Philadelphia, Pennsylvania, hand in hand, clutching shopping bags, Abdullah and Trish strolled out of the Franklin Mills Mall into the partially sunny and bitter air.

Happily, the pair chatted and laughed along together as they made their way through the Franklin Mills parking lot. The lovebirds climbed onto Trish's gray '88 Chrysler New York. Trish pulled off with ease, heading back to Delaware.

When Trish and Ebony attained their licenses, they traveled all over the tri-state area taking in the sights. Abdullah would always tag along with the two best friends. He often spent time with them exclusively, riding shotgun in their vehicles. And of course, Ebony was in the dark about Abdullah's and Trish's secret rendezvous. It had gotten to the point where Abdullah and Trish had fallen neck deep into their down-low teenage love affair; it was no turning back.

*****

The truth be told, Abdullah was playing the two best friends. He would always tell Trish that he didn't have any feelings for Ebony and yet at the same time toy with Trish's fragile conscious. "We can't hurt Ebony, we can't do dat to her. Maybe we should end it, you and me. I don't know, though, I love you to death. We can't end this, we love each other. We just gotta keep this between us 'cuz we don't wanna break Ebony's heart. You know what I'm saying?" he would slyly say.

Hours later, nightfall. Now in Delaware with Surface's "Closer Than Just Friends" blaring in her New Yorker, Trish hooked a right turn into a Red Lobster restaurant's parking lot.

"You're all I need in my life, don't need no one, don't need no one but you. Only you can make me happy, so happy," Trish sang elatedly, as she pulled into a parking spot, cutting the engine off, affectionately grabbing Abdullah's chin, searching his eyes.

Just as the young lovers departed Trish's New Yorker, Ebony emerged from the dark parking lot accompanied by her cousin Mischa.

"This is unbelievable, I don't fucking believe this! Abdullah, how could you do this to me. She's my best friend! Trish, why? You know I love him," Ebony exclaimed in dread with flamed eyes while she peered at Abdullah then Trish.

Abdullah tried to speak, but not a single word leaped from his mouth.

"Ebony I—"

Ebony cut Trish off. "Trish, I don't want to hear your excuses. How could you stoop so low and mess with my boyfriend behind my back? How could you? You know what? You can have his punk ass. I am finished with him! Abdullah, you had a good thing!" she lamented, as the tears commenced to drop from her eyes.

Crying uncontrollably, Ebony stormed away from the deceitful pair. Before following her cousin's footsteps, Mischa glared at Abdullah and Trish with repugnance.

Ebony, along with Mischa, climbed into her dark-green Oldsmobile. Animatedly, Abdullah rushed up to Ebony's vehicle.

"Ebony! Ebony! Ebony!" Abdullah hollered as he feverishly tapped onto the driver's side window.

Ignoring him as if he no longer existed, Ebony cut the engine on and backed out of her parking spot, coasting into the night, through the parking lot, sliding through the near exit, and jumping on the highway while encountering busy traffic.

Looking on, Abdullah displayed a half-regretful, pathetic facial expression. Although the darkness of the night concealed the anguish on Abdullah's face from Trish as she drew near.

"Abdullah?" Trish said quietly, burying herself into his arms.

"Don't worry about her, you got me, you got me. I tried to fix things up between y'all, but she kept going. She wasn't trying to hear nothing. We're all we need," Abdullah whispered into Trish's ear, patting her back.

Abdullah was lying through his teeth; he didn't care about Ebony and Trish's friendship. His agenda was solely to fulfill his needs, to have his cake and eat it too.

From the very moment that Abdullah and Trish were spotted together at Red Lobster, that was the very moment their secret teenage love affair became official. There was no longer a need for the pair to creep around. Their forbidden love was finally out of the hat.

A part of Trish was glad that she was caught red-handed with Abdullah. To her it was a burden to keep who she loved under wraps. The other part of her being felt bad about the fact that she stole her best friend's boyfriend. Although the love she had in the depths of her heart for Abdullah demolished the guilt of betrayal.

Three weeks had passed, and Ebony and Trish hadn't uttered a single word to one another. In their high school they would mosey right by each other as if they never met. In the history class they shared they wouldn't dare lay their eyes on one another. The tension between the two longtime ex best friends flustered as the days blew by. Mount Pleasant High was talking; whispers swarmed the hallways about Ebony and Trish. Who were among the popular people, not to mention the finest that strutted through the high school.

Some said they were lesbians having a quarrel; some said they weren't talking to each other because of a boy, but who was he? Ebony and Trish were tight-lipped about the whole situation. Others said Ebony was jealous of Trish and vice versa. Anything that you could think of that was mischievous was said about the two teenage girls.

Then one dreary, snowy night, out of the blue Trish received a phone call from Ebony.

"Hello?" Trish sang into the telephone, sitting in her bedroom.

"Hey, Trish," Ebony replied in a friendly tone, also lounging in her bedroom.

"Ebony?" Trish said in surprise.

"Yes, it's me. I am tired of all this nonsense. I am not gonna let Abdullah destroy our friendship. You are my best friend. Like I told you that night, you can have him. I'm cool. Besides, I have somebody else now. So let's just make up, okay? Let's put this behind us," Ebony said calmly.

"So what are we gonna do this weekend?" Trish asked before they both erupted in laughter.

And with that, Ebony and Trish were back to being best friends again.

Chapter 22

The following year, 1993, Abdullah sat in the back seat of a Lincoln limousine, as the driver pushed the limo through Claymont, Delaware. The driver pulled up to Trish's house and parked.

Sporting a white tuxedo, Abdullah hopped out of the limo and headed to Trish's house.

*****

"Abdullah, she'll be right down," Trish's mother said in a very pleasant manner, while Abdullah sat on the living room couch, as she departed the room.

Seven minutes later, Trish made her way down the steps, and strolled into the living room. An astounded Abdullah sprang off the couch onto his feet, scanning Trish's stunning dress inch by inch bottom to top, then their eyes met.

"Damn, Trish, you look good as hell," Abdullah proclaimed.

"You like my dress, Ab?" Trish replied, smiling, as she spun around.

Trish's mother strolled back into the living room with a camera.

"Come on, let me take y'all picture," Miss Jongnam said comfortably.

Eagerly, Abdullah took Trish by the hand and led her in front of the camera as Trish's mother leveled the picture machine. Abdullah roped his arm around Trish, anticipating a photograph. Stone-facing the camera while she smiled warmly. The flash from the camera filled the living room like a stormy night.

Trish slid in front of Abdullah for another picture, placing her backside against his body, while he planted his chin on her shoulder, wrapping his arms around her waist. The camera clicked as the light flashed, capturing the image of the young lovers.

Moments later, the young lovers headed for the front door while Trish's mother followed not far behind.

"Bye, Miss Jongnam," Abdullah said, stepping through the door as Trish also said bye to her mother, on the heels of her boyfriend.

"All right, you kids have fun, be good," Trish's mother said elatedly, standing in the doorway, waving to the teens while they walked to the waiting limo.

Abdullah held open the door of the limousine as Trish climbed into the vehicle. Then he waved to her mother, proceeding into the limo.

"Where to?" the chauffer asked, peering into the rearview mirror.

"Mount Pleasant High," Abdullah answered.

The driver took the limo out of the park, pulling off with ease. Abdullah popped a bottle of champagne and took a long swig.

"You want some of this bubbly?" Abdullah inquired before guzzling the bottle of Moët.

"I'm fine, baby," Trish said softly.

"Trish, this is our prom night," Abdullah replied.

"Ab, you know I don't drink," Trish said awkwardly.

"I know, but this is a special occasion, and it calls for a celebration," Abdullah said slyly, taking a sip from the Moët bottle. "Please, pretty please? Come on, Trish, live a little. One taste won't hurt. Come on, this is our prom, baby girl."

Trish sighed. "Okay, Abdullah, I'll try it. One taste, but only one taste," she said reluctantly, reaching for the champagne bottle.

Trish wrapped her lips around the Moët bottle and tilted it, as she fixed her eyes on Abdullah. After her little swig, Trish planted her soft lips onto the love of her life's lips.

Minutes later they arrived at Mount Pleasant High. The lovebirds climbed out of the limousine and made their way to the dance.

*****

"November Rain" by Guns N' Roses blared as Abdullah and Trish entered the gymnasium to be greeted by a sea of adolescents. The teenagers were dressed to kill, having the time of their lives.

Moments later, Whitney Houston's version of "I Will Always Love You" swam through the gym, while Abdullah and Trish slow danced, holding each other close. As Abdullah and Trish glided, embracing one another, Abdullah felt eyes molesting his face. He surveyed the crowd to find Ebony behind the eyes that stared like an owl, resting in her date's arms.

After the Whitney Houston cut ended, "It Must Have Been Love" by Roxette proceeded through the speakers, while Abdullah and Ebony continued to stare intensely through the crowd. Once the Roxette song faded, Ebony broke the gaze between her and Abdullah, bolting out of the gymnasium while her date looked on in disbelief.

Quickly, Abdullah whispered into Trish's ear, "I'm going to the bathroom."

Abdullah stepped out of the gymnasium into the hallway of Mount Pleasant High. Ebony stood in the corridor with tears in her eyes, waiting for Abdullah to approach her, just as she had predicted that he would come running.

"Abdullah, I must admit I was in love with you, but not anymore. I still have love for you even though you broke my heart. I guess we're not meant to be together. Let's just walk away from each other," Ebony said sadly as her tears poured down her face.

"Don't cry, Ebony. Listen, I'll make all this up to you. But yo, I need to know one thing. Who the fuck is dat clown?" Abdullah said, searching her misty eyes.

"That's none of your business. But hey, since you're all in my Kool-Aid, I'll let it be known. That clown is my boyfriend, and tonight I'm gonna give him my love, and I mean all of my love," Ebony ranted.

"Is dat right?" Abdullah replied with a smirk.

"Yes, that's right. What I am about to tell you will knock that smile right off your face," Ebony said sarcastically, whipping her neck side to side.

"What? Whatcha talking about?" Abdullah interrogated with a puzzled facial expression.

"I am talking about your girl Trish," Ebony retorted.

"What about Trish? Tell me!" Abdullah exclaimed, with fear invading his eyes.

"Abdullah, you have to give me your word of honor that you won't tell Trish that I told you," Ebony said bluntly.

"You got my word, now what is it? Tell me, what's the deal with Trish?" Abdullah said animatedly and worriedly.

"Abdullah, I'm only telling you this because I love you. I mean I'm not in love with you anymore, but I do care about you a little. You didn't hear this scoop from me. Remember, Trish is still my best friend." Ebony paused, searching his eyes. "She's playing you. She's seeing this guy named Vinny from West Chester."

Immediately, Abdullah's heart dropped, and his whole demeanor changed as the unbearable pain of infidelity sunk into his being, crumbling his world.

Ebony fought off the smile that sought desperately to form on her face, while she watched Abdullah hang his head, wallowing in his self-pity.

"Have a nice life, Abdullah! And after tonight, I never ever want to see your lowlife butt again," Ebony barked, waltzing back into the gymnasium.

Moments later, a shattered Abdullah mustered himself together and strolled back into the gymnasium to find Trish accompanied by Ebony, giggling, holding a conversation as "Weak" by SWV floated in the air.

Flaunting a monstrous facial expression, Abdullah encountered the two best friends.

"Hey, Ab," Ebony greeted, displaying a counterfeit smile, peering dead square into Abdullah's eyes. "It's been a while, so how you been?"

"I'm coolin', just chilling with my baby, you know?" Abdullah replied insolently, swinging his arm around Trish while the song "If I Ever Fall In Love" by Shai bounced from wall to wall throughout the gymnasium.

"Well, I am going to leave you guys alone, my boyfriend is waiting. I know he's probably having a fit," Ebony retorted, rolling her eyes at Abdullah and marching off, disappearing into the crowd.

"Ab, I think she's still heated. Oh well, she'll get over it. You're mine now, she can't stay mad forever, right?" Trish said calmly.

"Yeah, I guess so," Abdullah answered, concealing his sadness and anger.

*****

Abdullah held open the door of the limo, as Trish fell into the vehicle. Then he followed suit. Once inside the limousine, Abdullah turned to face Trish and stared coldly.

"We going back to her house," Abdullah informed the chauffeur, still glaring at Trish intensely.

"Hey, why are we going back to my house?" Trish questioned with a dumbfounded look.

"Trish, do you think I'm Tommy Tucker or something?" Abdullah scoffed.

"Who is Tommy Tucker?" Trish asked with a perplexed gaze.

"The neighborhood sucker! Listen, I know about you and Vinny!" Abdullah exclaimed, drowning the bottle of Moët.

"What in the world are you talking about?" Trish replied with a clueless facial expression.

"Vinny from West Chester," Abdullah barked, then he gulped the bottle of champagne.

"Who Vincent Marchant? I haven't seen him in years, since I was a little girl. When I lived up West Chester," Trish said solemnly.

"Kill the good girl act, let's just say I heard it through the grapevine about you two. Wining and dining, feeling fine you thought I would never find out, huh?" Abdullah said disdainfully.

"Well, whoever and whatever grapevine you heard that through is wrong. They are lying, Abdullah!" Trish said firmly.

"Did you fuck him? Don't lie, just tell me the truth," Abdullah said in despair, his voice leaping, filled with pain.

"This is truly unbelievable. You're the only one I've ever been with in my whole entire life, only you. I can't believe you're accusing me of cheating on you. Abdullah, I love you, don't you know that? I would never ever do anything to Jeopardize our love," Trish said with a candid facial expression.

Abdullah didn't reply to Trish. He just simply peered out of the limousine's window into the night as they sailed through Claymont, Delaware. Within minutes, the young teenage couple ended up in front of Trish's house.

"Abdullah, you can't believe everything you hear, you can't. You have to trust me. I never ever cheated on you, baby. I see you won't even look at me right now. I get it, you're mad. But know this: I do love you, and I always will. You hear me? When you cool off, call me. I'll be waiting," Trish said before she climbed out of the limo.

"You all right, young fellow?" the driver queried, looking into the rearview.

"Yeah, I'm straight. It ain't bout nuffin'. Yo! Drive up Philly. Matter fact, let's go up AC," Abdullah replied, pretending that his heart wasn't aching while the chauffeur slowly pulled off.

Abdullah didn't look back at Trish as they drove away into the night.

Cruising the streets of Atlantic City, New Jersey, viewing the glistening colors that the town exhibited, Abdullah reflected back to Trish right before she hopped out of the limo.

"Abdullah, you can't believe everything you hear, you can't. You have to trust me I never ever cheated on you, baby. You won't even look at me right now, I get it you're mad, but know this, I do love you, and I always will, you hear me? When you cool off, call me, I'll be waiting."

Abdullah snapped back to reality, shaking his head in confusion. *She might not be cheating on me*, he thought to himself.

*****

The following evening, at around six, Trish's mother stepped through the front door of her residence. "I'm home."

She shouted, "Trisha, we need to talk about what college you should attend."

Miss Jongnam toed up the staircase. Ultimately ending up in front of Trish's bedroom. Gently, she knocked on the door and eased her way into the bedroom to find her daughter lying in her bed on her side, wrapped chin deep in a comforter.

She must be hungover from last night, Trish's mother thought to herself, gazing down on her daughter who appeared to be sleeping peacefully.

"We'll talk when you get up," Miss Jongnam said in a tiny whisper, holding a smile.

Just as Trish's mother headed toward the bedroom door, she spotted a puddle of blood resting on the carpet near the wall. Filled with dismay, stopping in her tracks, she hustled back to Trish.

Violently, Miss Jongnam tore away the covers from the body of her daughter to make a frightening discovery. There lay Trish with her throat slashed ear to ear, along with her heart savagely ripped out of its cavity, with her blood decorating her white sheets.

Struck with horror and shock, eyes bulging, Miss Jongnam screamed at the top of her lungs: "Noooo! No, not my Trisha!"

Chapter 23

"Hi, I'm Detective Harry Moscicki."

"And I'm Detective Mark Johnson. We'll be working on solving your daughter's murder."

"Um, Miss Fennedy, there some questions we need to ask you. Did Trisha have a boyfriend?" Detective Harry Moscicki said as they sat in the living room while a team of badges went over the house inch by inch and foot by foot for evidence.

"Yes, his name is Abdullah Saladin. They went to the prom last night. Trish was so happy," Miss Jongnam replied as her voice cracked with emotion.

"Do you know where we can find Abdullah Saladin?" Detective Mark Johnson queried.

"No, but Trisha's friend Ebony Tatts might know. Her number is 798-9857," Miss Jongnam said falteringly as Detective Mark Johnson jotted down the information on a little tablet.

*****

Three hours later, at the New Castle County Police headquarters, a crew of homicide detectives were discussing intelligence they had gathered up concerning the murder of Trish.

Lieutenant Douglas Malvo stood behind a podium briefing the lawmen as he pointed toward a whiteboard that occupied a diagram of pictures of Abdullah, Jax, Trish, and Ebony. The diagram was square shaped; Jax and Trish's photographs were on the top with Abdullah and Ebony at the bottom.

"A few years back in 1991 I was investigating the Davis case, which as of today remains unsolved. Jax Davis was dating Trisha

Fennedy, Abdullah Saladin was dating Ebony Tatts. On August 3, 1991, Abdullah Saladin met up with Ebony Tatts, Jax Davis, and Trish Fennedy at the Elsmere skating rink. After skating they caught a taxi to Ebony Tatts's house in Claymont. Around 2:00 a.m., according to Abdullah Saladin, he received a page from a friend regarding a fight. The friend's nickname was Popbo. However, we were unable to find out Popbo's real name. Popbo summoned Abdullah Saladin and Jax Davis to meet him at the Claymont High racetrack, so they could fight a gang from Chester, Pennsylvania. Popbo never showed up at the racetrack. Although the gang from Chester did. Abdullah Saladin and Jax Davis were outnumbered by the gang so they fled. Abdullah Saladin made it back to Ebony Tatts's unharmed, Jax on the other hand was not so lucky. He returned to Ebony Tatts's house, bleeding profusely. Where he died in Trisha Fennedy's arms from multiple stab wounds to the abdomen. Ironically, now, Trisha Fennedy is the murder victim. In both murders a knife was used. It could be a coincidence that a knife was the murder weapon in both of the homicides, but my gut tells me different. Ebony Tatts, Abdullah Saladin's former girlfriend and the best friend of Trisha Fennedy, stated that she believes Abdullah Saladin is responsible for Trisha Fennedy's murder due to his jealousy over some guy he thought she was seeing on the side," Lieutenant Douglas Malvo relayed. "I'm not buying the Chester gang story."

"Maybe Abdullah Saladin killed Jax Davis so he could be with Trisha, then ultimately he thought she crossed him, so he killed her too in a jealous fit of rage," Detective Harry Moscicki theorized, sitting among his colleagues.

"Here's the thing. We have no witness to any of these murders or any physical evidence tying Abdullah Saladin to these crimes. It's all circumstantial, we need a confession," Lieutenant Douglas Malvo proclaimed.

*****

The following night in Wilmington, Delaware, Abdullah rocketed a '78 black Trans Am through the streets while "Dre Day" by Doctor Dre featuring Snoop Dogg blared from the speakers.

Pulling up at a stop sign on Twenty-Fourth and Washington, a heavyset man emerged from out of the shadows, smoothly approaching the driver's side of Abdullah's Trans Am. Abdullah pushed the pause button to the car radio and quickly rolled down the window.

"What's up, House?" Abdullah greeted the heavyset man standing outside his vehicle.

"I can't call it, you been down deuce-deuce?" House said calmly.

"Nah, dat's where I'm going at now," Abdullah replied.

"Shiiiiit, I'm with you," House said hurriedly.

"Come on," Abdullah fired back, seizing a firearm from the passenger seat, tucking the lethal weapon into his waistband. Subsequently, House fell into the passenger seat and Abdullah promptly peeled off.

"Yo, you crazier than a motherfucker!" House exclaimed as Abdullah wheeled the '78 black Trans Am toward Twenty-Second Street.

"Whatcha talking about, House?" Abdullah asked without removing his eyes from off the streets.

"Nigga, you all over the news, the papers and everything. You wanted for murder, and you still in Delaware driving around like you got no worries in the world," House marveled.

"Say what?" Abdullah said, flabbergasted, shell-shocked from what he just heard while his eyes bulged.

"They said you killed a girl from out Claymont. Ab, if I was you, I would be long gone away from here. For sure they gonna try to give you life or the penalty. I know you ain't trying to go to death row. Jet, man. Get the fuck out of Delaware," House said soberly.

Abdullah sighed. "I didn't even know I was wanted," he said in disbelief.

Abdullah dropped House off on the live corner of 22nd and Carter, sliding off 22nd that was clustered with street players. As Abdullah left the corner, moving up the block, his heart commenced to pound out of fear of being apprehended.

Anxiously, Abdullah hooked a left turn, leaving Carter street, launching up twenty fourth street. In a matter of minutes, Abdullah reached a stop sign at Twenty-Fourth and Lamotte, stopping in

153

his tracks while a car slowly proceeded past, rolling down Lamotte toward Twenty-Third Street.

Sitting at the stop sign, Abdullah looked to his right, to be greeted by a handful of hustlers who stood by the corner store. Then Abdullah peered into the rearview mirror to make an alarming discovery: flashing red and blue lights creeping from the bottom of Twenty-Fourth street. With a fleet of police cruisers racing up the block drawing near, Abdullah slammed his foot onto the accelerator, missiling up Twenty-Fourth street, sailing across the intersection of Market Street.

Abdullah darted up the hilly Twenty-Fourth Street, encountering the funeral home that lined the block along with a park and row homes where flocks of spectators idled in front of while a team of squad cars city and state aggressively pursued him.

From out of nowhere, from the black swarthy sky emerged a police helicopter jointing the adrenaline run chase. The ghetto bird stalked Abdullah's every move with its search light tracing him. Abdullah rounded the corner at 24th and Tatnall with the badges on his heels. Reaching the speed of 55 miles per hour, Abdullah zipped down the city's pavement. Flowing and clearing Twenty-Fifth and Tatnall, Twenty-Sixth and Tatnall, Abdullah bent a left turn on to Twenty-Seventh and Tatnall disregarding the one-way street recklessly jumping onto a curb clearly colliding into a row house.

Swiftly, Abdullah hopped out of the Trans Am and dashed to a nearby alleyway as the authorities closed in, seeking to capture the fugitive, while the screaming sirens echoed throughout the night air.

With law enforcement hot on his trail, Abdullah entered the alleyway coming face to face with a dime bread teenage girl who held wide and beautiful eyes, along with a tannish complexion.

"Melly, hold this," Abdullah said warily, as he slickly and discreetly planted his nickel-plated, pearl-handled .25 semiautomatic into the right back pocket of her jeans, then placing his street candy into her left back pocket feeling her butt.

Feverishly and passionately, Abdullah kissed Melly's top lip then her bottom lip as the badges advanced closer.

Abdullah threw Melly into his arms. "I'm not gonna hurt you, just play along, play it off," he whispered into her ear in desperation.

And with that, the authorities footed closer and closer toward Abdullah with their firearms drawn.

"Freeze!" one of the badges in the midst of his colleagues shouted, leveling his pistol at Abdullah.

Immediately, Abdullah spun behind Melly, digging his index finger into the small of her back as if he was clutching lethal weapon.

Abdullah was surrounded at the opposite end of the alleyway were posted an army of police officers barricading off a possible escape route for the wanted criminal, hindering his getaway.

"Let me go! If not, she gets it in the back. I'm not playing," Abdullah roared.

"Abdullah Saladin, you don't want to do this. Don't dig yourself a deeper hole, son, let the young lady go," the lawman said cautiously, aiming his firearm at Abdullah. Violently, Abdullah shoved Melly towards the badges and bolted. The lawmen gave chase after Abdullah. Through the alley, Abdullah trotted to the left, heading for the backyard that furnished the alleyway, proceeding pass garages. Coming upon a fence, with the authorities not far behind.

Promptly, Abdullah cleared the fence landing in a backyard. Abdullah sprinted through the yard with the badges inches away from his back.

In a matter of minutes, Abdullah raced out into the street of West Street to be greeted by an assortment of fire power the law enforcement brandished while the ghetto bird hovered from above.

With muzzles staring him down, Abdullah froze in his tracks, realizing that he was trapped, nowhere to run. Nowhere to hide, raising his hands to the sky surrendering.

And with that, handcuffs were slapped on to Abdullah. He was taken into custody, thrown into the back seat of a unmarked vehicle.

The authorities were so overzealous to apprehend Abdullah. They forgot all about the girl, Melly, who slyly slipped away into the night with Abdullah's tiny firearm and street candy.

*****

Moments later, in the New Castle County police station, Abdullah was escorted to a steel-bared room. Turn Key opened the steel barred door that was connected to a barred cage that stored many alleged felons. Abdullah stepped into the steel-barred room. Turn Key slammed the steel-barred door behind Abdullah. Subsequently, Abdullah eased his handcuffed hands into the little hole in the barred door as Turn Key inserted his key into his handcuffs. In a matter of seconds, Abdullah was out of the handcuffs.

Abdullah stepped deeper into the barred cage and scanned the mugs of the alleged felons to see if he recognized anyone. And sure enough, he did.

"Tariq Baltimore, what's happening?" Abdullah said with a half-smile.

"Hey, what's going on, little homey?" Tariq Baltimore replied.

"I'm going back to Arkansas to fight these murder raps. Come here, let me kick it with you, he added as he made a gesture with his head, leading Abdullah away from the other lawbreakers.

"They got me on some murder one shit," Abdullah proclaimed.

"I know, I know. Don't be talking about your case to nobody."

"I don't care who it is. You didn't make a statement to them pigs, did you?" the older, wiser, slicker Tariq Baltimore said earnestly.

"Nah," Abdullah fired back. Shaking his head.

"You gotta watch out for the rats and snitches. Dat's why it's important dat you don't speak a word about your case 'cuz them no good sons of whores will exaggerate, fabricate a good ole story to cut a deal with the prosecution. Them folks are gonna try to get you to talk. They want you to incriminate yourself. They gonna be saying shit like help yourself. We're trying to help you, it's all bullshit. Their goal is to build a case against you and take you to court to get a conviction. Them pilgrims don't care if you're innocent or not. They want us all in jail for real, for real... A lot of niggaz went down 'cuz they couldn't keep their mouths shut. Abdullah, when they come talk to you, you tell them fucking pilgrims pigs to kiss your ass, you want a lawyer, dat's all you say," Tariq Baltimore said sharply.

*****

"Abdullah Saladin, nice to meet you. Unfortunately, we had to meet on these terms, but it is nice to meet you. I'm Detective Harry Moscicki. I just need to ask you some questions about Trisha Fennedy, your girlfriend." The Detective smiled slightly. "Did you take Trisha to the prom?" he queried, sitting at a table with Abdullah as Detective Mark Johnson, Lieutenant Douglas Malvo, and Prosecutor Paris Crane stood outside the interview room observing the interrogation.

Abdullah provided no reply ignoring the homicide detective, looking on with a stone face.

"Where were you after the prom?" Detective Harry Moscicki threw another question at Abdullah.

Abdullah dropped his head again, ignoring the lawman's questions as Detective Mark Johnson abruptly entered the interview room, setting into a seat right next to his partner.

"How are you? I'm Detective Mark Johnson. Call me Mark. We're on your side. This mute game isn't getting you anywhere. We're giving you the opportunity to come clean and save yourself from the death penalty. Look, man, we know you were jealous. You thought Vincent Marchant was doing Trisha, but I'm gonna ease the pain a bit for you! Vincent Marchant wasn't doing her. She was faithful to you. Ebony lied about Trisha stepping out on you to break you guys up. See, you killed Trisha in vain. You gotta do right by her because you loved her, we know you didn't mean to kill her. It's all in your eyes that you want to tell us what happen. Do what's right, do right by her. Confess, tell us what happened, so you can save yourself. What really happen to Jax? We know the Chester guys didn't kill him, we're not fishing here. We have a witness that saw you kill Jax. Abdullah, you need help, and the only way we can help you is that you tell us what happen. Tell us why you killed Jax and Trisha, help yourself. You have a mental sickness that needs to be addressed. Abdullah, Trisha loved you so do right by her," Detective Mark Johnson said, striving to get Abdullah to talk, searching his eyes.

"If Abdullah Saladin doesn't confess he walks, it's all speculation, I need more and the hostage situation is useless, we have no victim to file kidnapping charges would be meritless," Prosecutor Paris Crane said with disappointment in her voice, peering at the homicide detectives who sought to fracture Abdullah, while she stood outside of the interview room with Lieutenant Douglas Malvo.

"I don't think he's gonna break, he hasn't said one single word since I laid my eyes on him," Lieutenant Douglas Malvo replied as he folded his arms staring at Abdullah.

"Your good friend Popbo gave you up. He told us how you bragged about killing Jax. You're going up the river unless you help yourself. Abdullah, tell us what happened so we can go talk to the prosecutor and put in a good word for you. We're trying to help you, but you gotta help yourself by telling us what happened," Detective Mark Johnson persuaded.

"I want a lawyer!" Abdullah said firmly.

Suddenly, Detective Mark Johnson pounded his fist against the table and stormed out of the interview room with his partner Detective Harry Moscicki in tow. Detective Mark Johnson, along with Harry Moscicki, stepped into the room where Lieutenant Douglas Malvo and Prosecutor Paris Crane observed Abdullah sitting in the cramped tiny interview room by his lonesome.

"Now what?" Detective Mark Johnson asked, aggravated, glancing at Lieutenant Douglas Malvo, then peering at Prosecutor Paris Crane while his partner Detective Harry Moscicki stood by his side.

"Resisting arrest is a misdemeanor. I suppose we're going to have to let Abdullah Saladin go. We have nothing to hold him on," Prosecutor Paris Crane said frustratingly, as her eyes scanned the lawmen one by one.

They don't got nothing on me. How they gonna say Popbo saw me off Jax when I made Popbo up, they don't got nothing. They fishing like a motherfucker, Abdullah thought to himself as he slightly grinned, staring at the table he sat at in the cramped tiny interview room.

*****

Later on that night, free as a bird. Abdullah strolled up to an apartment building. Carefully, looking around making sure that no one was tailing him. Abdullah, swiftly made his way through the complex. Now standing in front of the apartment building, Abdullah finger tapped the button to the intercom system. Quickly, a female's voice tore through the speakers.

"Who is it?"

"Abdullah!"

"Hold on, Ab."

A buzzing sound rang out.

Energetically, Abdullah grabbed the door and entered the apartment building, within a matter of minutes. Abdullah was facing apartment 702.

"Come in, Ab, I won't bite you," a female's voice danced behind the door sarcastically.

Abdullah let out a little sigh and entered 702 to find Melly smiling ear to ear. Melly bolted to Abdullah, tightly embracing him. Then she back stepped to read his facial expression, searching his eyes.

"What's dat for?" Abdullah said dumbfoundingly.

"Hold on, let me get your stuff," Melly replied, avoiding the question.

Moments later, Melly returned to the front room where Abdullah sat comfortably on a sofa. Melly handed Abdullah his nickel pearl-handled pistol and street candy while she settled right next to him on the sofa.

"Yo, Melly, turn to Channel 6. I'm trying to catch the news. You know I might be on there," Abdullah expounded.

Calmly, Melly pointed the remoted control at the television, switching the channel from HBO to ABC.

"A fugitive man who had been on the lam for seven years was captured today, Tariq Child. Formerly of Baltimore, Maryland, was wanted for nine counts of murder in Little Rock, Arkansas. He is a member of the notorious Crips Gang. He was featured on America's Most Wanted. A viewer of America's Most Wanted TV show recognized Child and called the authorities."

"Yo, I just left him," Abdullah declared, pointing at the television.

"Abdullah." Melly paused to make sure that she had his undivided attention while she turned the television off. "This might be the last time we see each other. We're moving back to Venezuela," she uttered as her eyes connected with Abdullah's.

"What? Moving? When?" Abdullah fired back with a surprised facial expression.

"In the morning, we'll be leaving," Melly said softly.

"Melly, I don't want you to go," Abdullah replied.

"Don't act like you care now, nigga, you hardly ever spend time with me. You stood me up when you was supposed to take me to the movies. Now dat I'm moving, you don't want me to go. You want to spend some time with me. You don't want me to move. Get a grip, Abdullah," Melly tongue-lashed.

"All right. All right, you right. I fucked up... You want something to eat? 'Cuz I'm hungrier than a motherfucker," Abdullah said, hurriedly changing the subject.

"It's eleven something at night, I already ate. Thank you, though. Do you want to stay with me, my last night in the States?" Melly said frankly.

Caught off guard by Melly's unexpected question, Abdullah slowly nodded yes.

"When my mom goes to sleep, we'll go to my room. Go ahead, get yourself something to eat here," Melly said calmly as she handed Abdullah her house key.

*****

Abdullah stepped out of Kennedy Fried onto the pavement of Thirtieth and Market Street. A '93 green Toyota Camry LE hooked a left turn at Thirtieth and Market pulling alongside of the Kennedy Fried establishment. It was Abdullah's longtime friend Vic and his crew from Thirtieth Street, Chubby, Thugsey, and H. The 3-0 street gang climbed out of the vehicle and made their way to Abdullah who stood on the side of the eatery.

"What's up, Ab?" Vic greeted, coming face-to-face with Abdullah, shaking his hand along with Chubby, Thugsey, and H, who followed suit.

After pulling on a blunt, Thugsey passed Abdullah the blunt subsequently lifting another perfectly rolled up blunt from his ear, smoothly lighting it, pulling softly.

"Yo, Vic, let me get a ride down 2-2," Abdullah said before he slowly inhaled the marijuana. "The Jakes took my Trans Am."

"Where the BMW at?" Vic queried.

"Shit the Jakes took dat a while ago CS got pulled over and got caught with a nine and some coke, ten bundles. I'm get the Trans Am back they didn't find shit," Abdullah replied.

Moments later underneath the glare of the streetlights off 22nd and Carter Vic pulled upon the corner. Before Abdullah departed the Toyota Camry, he pounded his fist against the fists of H, Thugsey, Chubby, and Vic. Vic missiled up Carter Street, disappearing into the darkness of the night.

Abdullah made his way toward a row house that sat near the corner. In front of the row home stood a group of street players passing a blunt back and forth among themselves while they waited on crack sales to flourish from out of the night.

Just as Abdullah stepped two feet away from the pack of hustlers, he was rushed by an avid crack fiend. Without any hesitation, Abdullah served the junkie, street candy for dead presidents. Then he toed to the street players.

"Ab, ain't no tic for tac tonight, the block is all you," one of the pushers from out of the group said as he nonchalantly handed Abdullah a freshly lit blunt, strutting off, dispersing along with the other street players.

Hours later, by his lonesome. Abdullah sat on the stoop of the row home near the corner of 22nd and Carter counting the stack of fluffy dead presidents that he accumulated from selling street candy. Shortly after, a squad car with its headlights out slithered up Twenty-Second street. Simultaneously, the white cop who wheeled the police cruiser and the black cop, his partner, and passenger intently surveyed the blank street for any illegal activities, for any open-air drug deals.

Approaching the corner, approaching the row house, the lawman's eyes landed on Abdullah. Abdullah stared back at the badges, not recoiling one bit as they sluggishly rolled past him.

Once the squad car reached the stop sign on Twenty-Second and Lamotte, up the block from Abdullah, Abdullah with his eyes glued on the patrol vehicle hopped up off the stoop.

The police cruiser froze at the stop sign, stalling for minutes, then abruptly bent a left turn, darting down Lamotte's street.

'They coming back around!' Abdullah uttered to himself as he raced to the front door of the row home in panic.

Frantically, Abdullah pounded on the front door. In a matter of seconds, the front door swung open. Swiftly, Abdullah bolted into the row house.

"Abdullah, what the hell is going on?" the light-skinned, heavyset woman queried with bugged eyes, while she shut the front door behind him.

"The police, they out there!" Abdullah exclaimed.

"Dat's gonna cost you," the light-skinned, heavyset woman replied.

Abdullah passed the lady a rock, and she shot him a look as if one stone wasn't good enough.

"I got you, Miss Roberta," Abdullah fired back, holding a smile, handing the light-skinned heavyset woman another rock. And with that, Miss Roberta rocketed up the stairs, disappearing into the house.

Anxiously, Abdullah planted his knees into the couch that sat directly in front of a window, pulling the shade to the side, peering out of the window, discovering two squad cars parked on the street along with lawmen toeing the pavement.

With their flashlights beaming, scattered in the street, the four uniformed policeman combed the block.

Abdullah sighed, flopping onto the couch, checking his watch, which read 4:30 a.m. Abdullah whipped out a bottle of Hennessy and took a swig, followed by another swig followed by another swig.

Abdullah awoke grasping his nickel-plated, pearl-handled .25 semiautomatic. "Got to be more careful," Abdullah said astoundingly, glazing at the pistol in his hand.

162

Animatedly, Abdullah fumbled through his pockets for his United States currency and street candy. In a matter of seconds, he seized his money and drugs, counting it. Realizing that it was all there, Abdullah sighed in relief.

Energetically, Abdullah slid the shade to the window to the side, only to be greeted by the brightness of the morning.

With Melly on his mind, Abdullah charged out of the row house, as a midnight-blue Volvo pulled up in front of the residence cranking Kool G Rap and DJ Polo's "On the Run."

A teenage girl with a golden complexion climbed out of the Volvo. She was Miss Roberta's daughter, Wanda. She made her way to her house, proceeding past Abdullah.

"Pookie, let me get a ride up Twenty-Eighth Street," Abdullah said, looking down on the twentysomething-year-old man, who sat comfortably behind the wheel of the midnight-blue Volvo.

"Come on," Pookie quickly replied.

*****

Fearing that he had dropped the ball with Melly, Abdullah coasted through the hollow halls of her apartment building, eventually coming upon 702.

Clutching the key that Melly had gave him earlier, Abdullah inserted the key into the lock of the door as his hand shook uncontrollably. In the blink of an eye, Abdullah entered to find an empty apartment, Melly was gone as far as the eye could see.

Abdullah hung his head with deep regret.

Moments later, Abdullah stood at a telephone booth, listening to Melly's voice-mail messages.

"Abdullah, where are you? Where are you? Why aren't you here yet? Abdullah, it's getting real late. Bring your ass on. Abdullah, call me right now! Abdullah, it's six in the morning. I guess you don't want to see me, bye. Call me, hurry up!"

Chapter 24

Fast-forward back to the winter of 1994, Abdullah stepped into the Chinese store on Twenty-Fourth and Market as Pretty followed suit, inches away from his longtime friend.

Abdullah and Pretty sat on a ledge in the Chinese eatery with their backs leaning up against the fiberglass windows that hugged the Asian establishment.

Abdullah cracked open a blunt cigar, spilling the tobacco on to the floor. Artfully, he sprinkled the spinach that lead to Shyba's doom into Philly blunt. Then he wrapped and licked the blunt cigar, molding it flawlessly.

Subsequently, Abdullah lit the blunt cigar, inhaling and exhaling. The aroma from the marijuana and smoke wandered through out the Chinese store as Abdullah puffed away nonchalantly. A man waltzed into the Asian establishment.

"Abdullah, let me get two bags of dat kill," the man said, standing in front of Abdullah and Pretty holding a crisp twenty-dollar bill.

Quickly, Abdullah pulled out a sandwich bag that contained a heap of dime bags stuffed with skunk. Abdullah snatched two dime bags while his lips grasped the blunt cigar, handing the sacks to the weed buyer, who passed him a crisp twenty-dollar bill.

The Chinese were unconcerned about the drug transactions and the reefer that was being inhaled on the daily in their eatery. Some might say they had a little appreciation for the law. After all they would hold and conceal drug packages for some of the hustlers and Abdullah and Pretty were in that circle.

When the heat was on, when the narcs would descend on Twenty-Fourth Street in anticipation of making a drug bust, the pushers trapped in the Chinese store often sidestepped the raids by slyly slinging their street candy over the counter to Chad.

Young Buck Jones accompanied with young Bushwick entered the Asian establishment. The four footers greeted Abdullah and Pretty before they sat across from them on the other side of the entrance way on the ledge.

Abdullah rose from off the ledge, making his way to the youngsters, handing Buck Jones the blunt cigar. Calmly, Buck Jones took his pulls, inhaling, exhaling, passing the doobie to Bushwick, who wasted no time to let the marijuana seep into his lungs.

Pretty's pager erupted: b*eep, beep, beep, beep.*

And with that, Pretty strolled out of the Chinese store, stepping onto the pavement, making his way to the pay phone. Pretty drummed the numbers to the pay phone. The pay phone rang three times before a voice eased on to the line.

"Hello?" Brooke sang.

"What's up, Brooke?" Pretty replied energetically.

"Pretty where you at?" Brooke pried.

"I'm on 2-4," Pretty divulged.

"We need to talk, baby," Brooke said soberly.

"All right, I'm on my way, you hungry?" Pretty said gently.

"Yeah I'm hungry. Get me seven chicken wings, two egg rolls, and an ice tea Mistic. I love you," Brooke fired back.

"I love you too," Pretty proclaimed.

*****

Moments later. Pretty sat with Brooke in the kitchen of her row home, while she greedily torn the skin from the chicken limb from limb. Upon finishing her chicken, then downing her ice tea Mistic, Brooke eyed Pretty who sat quietly.

"Pretty," Brooke paused to make sure she had his full attention. "I'm pregnant, baby, we're having a baby!" she announced in a joyous tone.

Simultaneously, Pretty and Brooke rose from out of their seats, embracing one another.

*****

As Detective Pitt sat at his desk in the comfort of Robbery, Homicide Division, Detective Ortiz smoothly approached.

"The prints that were on the safe belong to Shaman and Carolyn Wilson," Detective Ortiz said plainly as he handed Detective Pitt a piece of paper.

"What about leads do we have any?" Detective Pitt queried.

"We don't have any, nobody's talking on this one," Detective Ortiz said dryly, flopping into a seat at his desk.

Later on in the nightfall of Wilmington, Delaware, Abdullah, Pretty, Crack, Young Buck Jones, Ed-Lover, Flock, Rog, CS, and Young Bushwick dwelled in the Chinese store on Twenty-Fourth and Market Street. Three blunt cigars rotated through the hands of the hustlers with exception of Pretty who simply looked on in the smoked-out eatery.

Abruptly, Monifah bolted into the Asian establishment.

"Abdullah, why aren't you answering my pages?" Monifah ranted.

Without any hesitation, Abdullah roped his arm around Monifah, ushering her out of the smoke-infested store into the darkness under the glistening streetlights.

"What's wrong, Mo?" Abdullah asked.

"Abdullah, I just wanted to hear your voice, I wanted to talk to you, I've been paging you for the last two hours," Monifah replied with frustration in her eyes.

"Mo, my pager was off," Abdullah justified, displaying his loot clocker, switching it on. "Go back down Brooke's, I'll be down the crib later on," he added as they strolled down Market Street.

Shoulder to shoulder, Abdullah and Monifah toed past liquor stores and eateries. The couple bent a right around a corner, proceeding into Concord Avenue.

The streetlights glared down on Abdullah and Monifah as they cuddled while the oncoming traffic and outgoing traffic faced pass them. Some noticed the embracing pair, some didn't.

Shortly after, Abdullah marched across Twenty-Second and Market Street, heading up the strip as Pretty made his way down Market Street. Abdullah and Pretty bumped heads right in front of an alley way, a narrow street that sat between Twenty-Second Street and Twenty-Third Street.

"Where you going, dog?" Abdullah queried.

"Brooke's, my baby mommy, I knocked her the fuck up," Pretty declared animatedly, smiling ear to ear.

Chapter 25

Two weeks later, a '94 money-green, rimmed-up land cruiser with tinted windows rolled up Twenty-Second Street as the rain fell from the grayish sky striking everything it came in contact with. The money-green Land Cruiser pulled up on Twenty-Second and Lamotte where Abdullah stood near by a row home underneath an umbrella he clutched along with Mone, Munch, and South, who were also seeking refuge under their umbrellas. Lively, Pretty climbed out of the money green Land Cruiser, As he made his way to Abdullah; Pretty greeted him and the other street player who accompanied him.

"Take a ride with me," Pretty said with a smile.

"Now the funeral is over, and all the tears are dried up. Niggaz hanging deep on the cut getting fired up, looking for the nigga who pulled a pistol on my homie, eye for an eye, and now your life is what you owe me." Scarface danced in the money-green Land Cruiser as Pretty whipped the SUV through the City of Wilmington, Delaware, with Abdullah slouching in the passenger seat.

"I'm ready, my paper is right. I'm trying to grab a bird, put me down with your Florida connect," Abdullah said candidly.

"All right, I got you, dat's what I'm talking about. Let's clock these geez, skies the limit. Twenty thousand dollars is the price for one key. You'll get fronted another one, dat's if you want it. Ab, I'm putting you down with the Florida connect. Don't try no ho shit, for real, it's time to get this paper. Fuck robbing niggaz, it ain't no need for dat. Dat brings heat, and it ain't no need for you to be on the block anymore. I'm done playing the block, front lining it is dead. I was greedy, but when Brooke told me she was pregnant, I realized dat I don't need to be out there like dat I'm just gonna sell weight now, lay low, you know? Dat's what you need to do, what happen to dat white girl from out Claymont?" Pretty said solemnly.

"Who Amanda?" Abdullah replied with uncertainty in his voice.

"Yeah, the girl who was saying she wasn't white, she's Italian and Puerto Rican, don't call her white girl, her!" Pretty confirmed as he glanced at Abdullah then focused his eyes back on the streets.

"She still stay out Claymont, she paged me the other day," Abdullah fired back.

"We gonna need her to bring the birds back, her and one of her white girls," Pretty informed. "You know the police ain't gonna fuck with the white girls like dat."

"I'll handle dat, Amanda will do anything for me," Abdullah assured, staring out of the passenger-side window, "Yo take me to my car, it's up Fortieth Street. I'm get on dat right now."

*****

Later on, in Claymont, Delaware, Abdullah shoved his '85 black beat-up Chevrolet Impala up Philadelphia Pike through the piercing rainstorm while Spicel's "A Trigger Gots No Heart" from the Menace II Society soundtrack thumped from the car radio speakers.

Staring into the rearview mirror, Abdullah spotted a state trooper squad creeping through the traffic.

Quickly, Abdullah turned down the music with his eyes glued to the rearview mirror as his heart commenced to beat violently. The state trooper flashed his lights as he aggressively skipped and dipped in between vehicles, drawing near the rear of Abdullah's Impala. In a matter of seconds the state trooper was right behind Abdullah, bumper to bumper. Seconds later, abruptly, the state trooper switched lanes, speeding past Abdullah, who immediately let out a sigh, while glancing at the firearm that rested in his waistband.

Shortly thereafter, Abdullah eased up into a shopping center, breezing through the parking lot, gliding into a parking spot.

Abdullah stepped into a pharmacy (Happy Harry's) to discover a teenager girl standing behind the counter of the establishment. She flaunted a baby-powder complexion, jade-green eyes with dark brown hair, exhibiting pleasing features. As soon as she noticed Abdullah she lit up like a Christmas tree smiling warmly displaying her dimples.

"Hey, Abdullah! I'll be on my break in five minutes, okay?" Amanda said cheerfully.

"I'm go across the street to McDonald's, you want something?" Abdullah said plainly.

"I'm fine, thank you," Amanda replied politely.

Abdullah and Amanda sat in Abdullah's '85 black beat-up Chevrolet Impala, while the rain pounded the vehicle.

"Amanda, let's go to Florida? What's up? You down?" Abdullah said gleefully as he proceeded to take a bite out of the Big Mac he held.

Surprised by what she just heard, Amanda tilted her head, squinting her eyes.

"Oh my God, okay. I'm with that, but when?" Amanda said, dumbfounded.

"Next week. Listen, I'm gonna need you to bring something back for me," Abdullah said, nipping at his burger.

"Abdullah? What do you want me to bring back, huh?" Amanda wisecracked, then she dug her hand into Abdullah's McDonald's bag, removing fries and tossing them into her mouth.

"What do I do to get money?" Abdullah retorted.

"Okay, so you want me to bring your drugs back… Yes, I'll do it, but only because you want me to because I like you," Amanda fired back, smiling ear to ear.

"Listen, here's what we're gonna do," Abdullah said calmly.

*****

Miami, Florida, a week later in the Holiday Inn in a plushy room, Abdullah sat restlessly by the telephone anticipating a phone call from the Florida connection, while Pretty watched the television nonchalantly.

Minutes later the telephone erupted. Animatedly, Abdullah snatched up the receiver.

"Hello?" he sang.

"Abdullah? What are you up to?" Amanda said in a hyper tone, sitting on a bed in a plushy room down the hall from Abdullah and Pretty accompanied with her friend Beth, who sat in a chair across from her, cracking her gum, staring in her mouth.

"Yo, I'll call you back," Abdullah said hurriedly.

"Is it cool for me and Beth to go to South Beach," Amanda asked softly.

"Yeah, go head, I'll see you at the beach," Abdullah replied.

Moments later, the telephone rang, this time Pretty scooped it up, "Hello?" he said.

"I'll be there tonight at twelve," the man on the line announced.

*****

Pretty wheeled a rented Maxima through the sunny streets of Miami, Florida, with Abdullah riding shotgun. The lawbreakers took in the view of scores of lady dime breeds, strutting the pavements along with sports cars and luxury cars sailing through the road beds, accompanied with palm trees decorating the blocks sitting gracefully underneath the blue sky.

Abdullah and Pretty marched through the almost-packed beach, earnestly searching for Amanda and Beth. Within a matter of minutes, the pair encountered the teenage girls. Soaking up the warmth of the sun, Amanda and Beth laid belly first on their towels clad in their bikinis.

Amanda and Beth had no idea that Abdullah and Pretty stood above them. Grinning devilishly, Abdullah vigorously smacked Amanda's butt. Immediately Amanda bounced up off her stomach to find Abdullah behind the slap, laughing uncontrollably.

"Abdullah!" Amanda shouted, as she lunged toward Abdullah who darted off into the beach.

Amanda gave chase after Abdullah as if they were playing a game of tag. Beth sat up with her rear resting against the floor of her towel with her arms roped around her bent knees.

171

"Why are you standing over there? Come here, what are you afraid of? Come here," Beth said boldly, looking up at Pretty, who stood calmly.

"Listen to you," Pretty fired back amused, slightly smiling, shaking his head as if he couldn't believe his ears.

"What? You don't mess with white girls?" Beth questioned with a puzzled facial expression.

"No, no, dat ain't it," Pretty asserted, pausing for a few seconds. "I got a girl, and she's having my baby. If we would have met earlier, it would have been on, but now dat my girl is carrying my seed I gotta keep it real with her."

"What your girl don't know won't hurt her," Beth retorted.

"But I will... I can't do dat to her and the 'baby,' you know what I'm saying?" Pretty said pointedly, peering deep into the windows of Beth's eyes.

"So what is this girl's name?" Beth snapped sarcastically.

"Her name is Brooke," Pretty sang, displaying a smile, removing his eyes from Beth, swiftly placing them on Abdullah and Amanda, who played in the shoreline while the waves from the ocean crashed down on the lovers' ankles.

As the clock struck 12:00 a.m., Abdullah and Pretty sat at a table in their plushy hotel room engaging in the card game of spades.

Several minutes later, the door to the plush room begun to throb with knocks. With that, Pretty rose from his seat, quickly making his way to the door.

"Who is it?" Pretty inquired, standing in front of the peek hole in the door, as Abdullah drew a firearm from his waistband, cocking the lethal weapon, throwing a bullet into the chamber, sliding the small cannon back into his waistband.

"Federico," the man on the other end of the door replied.

Quietly, Pretty turned to face Abdullah and smiled, shaking his head then opening the door. Federico entered the plushy room along with two other men.

Federico displayed a tan complexion as did the men who accompanied him. Amicably, Pretty and Federico shook hands. Then Pretty lead Federico and the men with him to the table where Abdullah sat.

Simultaneously, the drug suppliers tossed duffel bags onto the table. They unzipped the duffel bags, revealing kilos of cocaine.

The drug suppliers flaunted twelve bricks, ten for Pretty, two for Abdullah. Smoothly, Pretty placed a suitcase onto the table swinging the box open revealing every bit of 120,000 dollars.

"It's all there," Pretty guaranteed.

"I trust you we have been doing business for quite some time now," Federico said comfortably.

Pretty copped five kilos from the Florida connection for a hundred grand, and they fronted him five kilos. Abdullah, on the other hand, bought a kilo for twenty grand and was also fronted a kilo.

*****

Toting the street candy they had just obtained, Abdullah and Pretty stepped into Amanda and Beth's room to be greeted by the cut "Freak Like Me," sang by Adina Howard. Without any hesitation the lawbreakers stashed the kilos of cocaine.

"Ab, why don't we take a shower?" Amanda suggested.

"Come on!" Abdullah replied animatedly, bolting to the bathroom.

Once they were inside the bathroom, Abdullah and Amanda vigorously lip-locked as if they were wild animals.

*****

"Well, well, it's just you and me again. Come here, baby," Beth said, slickly and openly, flashing a smile, patting the bed she sat on while she shot Pretty a seductive gaze.

Pretty sighed, shaking his head.

Meanwhile, "Me and My Bitch" by Biggie Smalls mingled with the screams and moans that Amanda crowed from Abdullah, driving his manhood into her love tunnel from the back as he barbarically pulled her hair.

*****

"Tell Abdullah I went back to the room. All right?" Pretty said, before he headed to the door to leave.

"You sure you don't wanna lay up with me?" Beth chided with a half-smile, leaping off the bed and making her way toward Pretty.

Speechless, Pretty froze at the door as if it was a struggle to leave from the temptation, while he lifted his head, peering up at the ceiling of the hotel. Then he pulled open the door. And with that Pretty was gone.

Days later, early in the morning around nine something. Abdullah sat on the telephone with Amanda while Beth packed their bags, making preparation for them to travel back to Delaware.

"Make sure you stay on the speed limit. Listen, as soon as I get to Delaware, I'll be by your crib. Lay low, be cool, chill, go to work. I'm not gonna talk you to death. I'ma let you go. Remember, no speeding," Abdullah said soberly.

"I love you, Abdullah," Amanda proclaimed with emotion in her voice, immediately slamming the telephone in his ear disconnecting the line afraid he didn't feel the same way, afraid that he wouldn't return his love.

"Amanda! Amanda!" Abdullah hollered into the receiver shocked by her declaration.

Realizing that the line was dead, Abdullah hung up.

*****

Claymont, Delaware

Several days later, Abdullah and Pretty jumped out of Pretty's '94 money-green, rimmed-up Land Cruiser. They made their way to Amanda's house.

Eagerly, Abdullah planted three knocks on to the front door. A few minutes flew by before Amanda appeared, letting Abdullah and Pretty into her residence.

"Who here?" Abdullah pried, surveying the house as him and Pretty toed deeper into Amanda's dwelling. "Your mom here?"

"No, I'm all alone," Amanda replied.

Restfully, Pretty slouched on a couch in the living room while Abdullah and Amanda lingered in her bedroom.

"Here you go," Amanda said gently, as she handed Abdullah two duffel bags.

"Damn right!" Abdullah exclaimed, grabbing the bags.

"Abdullah," Amanda sang, pausing, searching his eyes as if she was seeking to read them. "Never mind."

Amanda wanted to know where her, and Abdullah stood in their relationship. She wanted to know how he felt about her, but she couldn't work up the nerve to ask.

*****

Clutching a duffel bag, Pretty waltzed into Brooke's row home with his friend Abdullah on his heels, who also held a duffel bag.

"Pretty, where the hell have you been?" Brooke ranted as she sprang from the love seat she occupied.

"Calm down, chill, I had to take care of some business," Pretty replied, displaying his duffel bag proudly.

"You and Abdullah have been missing in action for almost two weeks, gone in the wind, and you expect me not to be heated? You probably was with one of your whores," Brooke barked, storming off, proceeding to the steps.

"Brooke, hold up!" Pretty yelled, as he chased after her up the stairs.

Feverishly, Brooke raced to her room, slamming the door behind her while tears fell from her eyes. Within seconds, Pretty entered the bedroom to find a sobbing Brooke, sitting on the bed cupping her face with her hands. Pretty made his way to Brooke settling right next to her. Slowly, peeling her hands from off her face.

*****

Monifah rushed down the steps to be greeted by a relaxed Abdullah, who sat on a couch with a duffel bag sitting on the side of him on the floor.

In a blink of an eye, Monifah stood in front of Abdullah with her hands resting on her hips, peering down on him with fire in her eyes.

"What?" Abdullah uttered with raised eyebrows.

"What do you mean what? Boy—"

Abruptly, Abdullah cut Monifah off.

"Mo, I know what you're thinking, and it ain't like dat. You see this?" Abdullah expounded, unzipping his duffel bag, extracting a kilo, flaunting his street candy. "I got this for twenty stacks. I had to go to Florida to get this. I couldn't tell you I was leaving. I mean, couldn't tell nobody, dat's how niggaz get knocked, telling mother-fuckers and before they know, the Jakes know what's going down."

*****

"Brooke, I'm not playing you. Everything I'm doing is for us. I can't sell drugs forever. As soon as I make a million, I'm out the game. I love you and only you. You're gonna be the mother of my child. It's all about you and our baby, fuck them bitches! You know every time I make moves, I always do it differently, I know what it is. It's your hormones from being knocked up. They're going crazy, ain't they? You're probably worried about getting all fat and shit. If you blew up to 250, I'll still love you, I won't leave you," Pretty said sincerely, adding a little humor, grabbing Brooke's chin and looking deep into the windows of her eyes.

"Pretty, you know what? I can't even stay hot with you," Brooke fired back as her frown and tears slowly transformed into a slight smile while she took little sniffs, wiping her face.

*****

"Ab, it better be all about me 'cause, it's all about you. I'm keeping it real with you. You know I love you," Monifah said firmly.

The very next day, Abdullah and Pretty distributed their candy, flooding the streets of Wilmington, Delaware.

Seven months later, on a sunny day, sitting behind the wheel of his '95 gold Lexus Es300, Abdullah rocketed up Market Street as the cut "Life's A Bitch," by Nas and AZ roared from the speakers.

Abdullah pulled over on Market Street, parking between Twenty-Third Street and Twenty-Fourth street. Shutting down the engine, Abdullah climbed out of the gold Lexus to be greeted by Shimmey and Rivey (street players) who stood posted on the sidewalk, making open air crack sales while they nonchalantly clutched Heineken bottles.

"What up, Ab?" Shimmey exclaimed, as he shook Abdullah's hand.

"What's going on, black?" Rivey said with a smile, showing his pearly whites, extending his arm and shaking Abdullah's hand. "You want something to drink?" he added.

"Hell yeah," Abdullah replied.

And with that, Rivey made his way to his '95 gray BMW 325i that was parked in front of Abdullah's gold Lexus.

Swinging open the door to the Beemer, Rivey inclined into the vehicle. Within a matter of seconds, he backed out of the BMW with a cold bottle of Heineken, handing it to Abdullah.

Quickly, Abdullah cracked the lid to the brew, pouring the liquor on the pavement.

"This is for the cats who ain't here," Abdullah declared, before he took a swig.

While Abdullah, Shimmey, and Rivey conversed, Sami along with Joan bopped up Market Street, encountering the street players.

"Hey, Ab," Sami greeted.

Without uttering a single word, Abdullah nodded.

"What's your name, sexy?" Shimmey queried smoothly.

"Joan," she said softly.

"Okay now, okay now, my name is Shimmey," he said.

"I gotta take care of something. I'm out," Abdullah announced making his way to his '95 gold Lexus Es300.

Sami followed Abdullah not far behind as he climbed into the vehicle. While Abdullah inserted a key into the ignition, Sami eased into the passenger seat. Immediately, the Lexus came alive.

Meanwhile, Joan dug into her purse, retrieving a piece of paper that contained her telephone number. She passed her handle to Shimmey and walked off to Abdullah's vehicle, seductively throwing her money maker as if it were a salt shaker.

Before Joan flopped into the back seat of the '95 gold Lexus Es300, she looked back at Shimmey and smiled ear to ear.

Abdullah tapped the horn, pulling off with ease, waving to Shimmey and Rivey.

"Sugar Hill" by AZ featuring Miss Jones pounded out of the car speakers while Abdullah darted through the streets of Wilmington, Delaware.

Moments later, Abdullah slid into a parking spot, turning down "Mo Money, Mo Murder (Homicide)" by AZ, featuring Nas.

"Ab, I only got four hundred," Sami informed from the passenger seat, handing Abdullah a knot of dead presidents. "I'll make it up to you, though."

"You all right, you don't gotta make it up to me. Don't worry about it, it's only fifty dollars," Abdullah replied, holding a smile.

Abdullah departed the gold Lexus, strolling up the street, sipping liquor from the Heineken bottle he clutched, swiftly disappearing from out of Sami and Joan's sight.

Five minutes later, Abdullah returned hopping back into his '95 gold Lexus Es300, handing Sami a Ziploc Lock bag that contained a half ounce of street candy.

With Tupac Shakur's "Lord Knows" roaring from out of the Lexus speakers, Abdullah pulled up in front of Sami's house. Simultaneously, Sami and Joan jumped out of the gold Lexus.

"You coming in? Spend some time with me. Chill, let's chill," Sami said soberly, standing near the passenger side of the gold Lexus, peering into the vehicle, gazing at Abdullah who turned down the car radio.

"Nah, I gotta take care of something. I'm chilling," Abdullah said hesitatingly. "Holler at me when you off dat half," he added as he peeled off.

Later on as the sun proceeded to set, Abdullah stood at a telephone booth on Twenty-Third and Market Street, chatting it up with Monifah.

"I'll be here to get you at eight thirty," Abdullah related, observing the traffic zooming up and down Market Street.

The clock struck 8:25 p.m. as Monifah hawked the window from Pretty and Brooke's house in a middle-class neighborhood that was located on the outskirts of the city of Wilmington. Minutes later, at 8:29 p.m., Abdullah appeared in front of Pretty and Brooke's home in his '95 gold Lexus Es300. Abdullah drummed the horn to the steering wheel. Before Abdullah could blink, Monifah stepped out of the house, toeing toward him. Monifah slid into the passenger seat, leaning over to Abdullah planting her lips on his.

Immediately, Abdullah pulled off as Alexander O'Neil's "Sunshine" flooded the gold Lexus.

Moments later, the lovers made their way into a decent restaurant.

Once they came upon a table that sat in the corner of the establishment, swiftly, Abdullah pulled out a chair from the table for Monifah. Beaming uncontrollably, Monifah settled into the chair. Then Abdullah positioned himself into a seat across from Monifah. A waiter from the other end of restaurant hustled her way to the happy pair.

Later on that night, about ten something, Abdullah's hideout somewhere on the north side of Wilmington, he fumbled through a crate that contained a large amount of cassettes. Sitting on the bed tensely, Monifah watched Abdullah carefully as he came across what he was searching for. Slowly, Abdullah inserted a tape that consisted of slow cuts into the tape deck of a radio while the windows of his eye's displayed love and lust.

Hi-Five's "I Can't Wait Another Minute" invaded the room as Abdullah made his way to Monifah, easing in between her legs, pressing his body against hers, causing her to lay back first on the bed.

With Monifah's arms clinging to Abdullah's back, he violently kissed her lips, then her face, then her lips while she tried to keep up with his storm of kisses, kissing him back.

Abdullah ceased the kissing game, pulling Monifah's shirt off, removing his slowly sliding his tongue down.

Gazing into Monifah's eyes, Abdullah trailed his tongue back to her chest, snatching her bra from her perfectly shaped titties. He tongued and sucked her melons, placing them in his mouth one by one. Then he drove his tongue back down her stomach, coming upon the waistline of her dress. Intensely, their eyes locked from the anticipation and passion of becoming one slowly, Abdullah rose from the waistline of Monifah's dress not abandoning her eyes. He froze for a matter of seconds before he licked and kissed his way to her kneecap. He walked his tongue up her thigh as his hand caressed her other thigh. Abdullah maneuvered his hand underneath her dress, sliding his tongue across her inner thigh, approaching her panty line, licking all around the garment that shielded her warmth. Then he pulled her panties to the side, jabbing her wetness and tightness with his finger. After finger-popping her, he inserted his tongue into her love tunnel, sucking and licking her box.

Abdullah emerged from underneath Monifa's dress, throwing his tongue down her throat as the cut "Do you mind if I stroke you up, I don't mind. Do you mind if I stroke you down, I don't mind," by Changing Faces swam through the bedroom.

Feverishly, the horny pair disrobed the remainder of their clothes, with Monifah on her back, legs in the air. Abdullah artfully slid his manhood into her kitty cat. She clawed and dug her hands into his back as she slightly eased back from the penetration he waged.

SMV's "You're Always on My Mind" lingered in the air while Abdullah thrust into Monifah's love box.

A handful of minutes of Abdullah pounding Monifah's insides went by before they switched positions. Now with Abdullah stabbing Monifah from the rear, he grabbed and smacked her money maker.

"Don't cum in me," Monifah crowed, exploding in pure ecstasy from Abdullah drilling his manhood into her wet-blooded love tunnel. Subsequently, Abdullah unleashed his load into Monifah's womb.

Hours later, Monifah rested her head against Abdullah's bare chest as his arms embraced her tightly while they slept quietly and peacefully. Then suddenly the telephone erupted: *ring, ring, ring, ring, ring.*

Monifah awoke, rolling over to the left side of the bed, grabbing the receiver to the telephone cradle from the nightstand.

"Hello?" Monifah said weakly.

"Mo, let me speak to Ab," Pretty said anxiously.

Monifah reached over to Abdullah, shaking him with her hand. "Abdullah, Pretty's on the phone."

Animatedly, Abdullah hopped up and snatched his 9mm from underneath his pillow.

"Chill. Chill, Ab, it's Pretty. He's on the phone," Monifah said with panic in her voice with wide eyes.

Realizing that he was overreacting, Abdullah gathered himself together before scooping the telephone.

"Yo" Abdullah sang into the receiver.

"Sami just got knocked. One Time caught her with some coke on 2-7," Pretty notified.

*****

Meanwhile, at the Wilmington police headquarters, Sami sat handcuffed to a hard, cold steel chair by her lonesome. Moments later, a lone ivory-complexioned man draped in plain clothes entered the room where Sami was held as prisoner.

"You're facing a substantial amount of time behind bars, unless you have some information like who's your supplier. If you give me that, we can forget all about your charges," the lawman expounded.

"All right, all right," Sami said abruptly, peering at the narc who sat across from her at the other end of the table.

"Abdullah Saladin," she dropped the dime.

"Abdullah Saladin? The one who was a suspect in the murders of Trisha Fennedy and Jax Davis?" the lawman said with surprise in his voice.

"Uh-huh, he's the one who gave me the half ounce. He told me dat he killed Trisha and Jax. He was bragging about it too, talkin' 'bout how he got away with the murders, and y'all would never catch him," Sami divulged.

The very next day Sami was spotted riding around with the law in the passenger seat of a gray Lumina. The news spread like a wildfire all throughout the city of Wilmington. Everybody knew, streets were talking with the exception of Abdullah, who was in the dark.

As Abdullah wheeled his '95 gold Lexus Es300 through the streets of Wilmington with Tupac Shakur's "Str8 Ballin'" blasting from the speakers. His loot clocker commenced to leap inside his pants pocket. With one hand on the steering wheel, Abdullah snatched his pager from his pocket, scanning the screen of the beeper, which read 24-911-24-911.

Immediately, Abdullah found a pay phone. Abdullah climbed out of the vehicle and made his way to the telephone booth, animatedly slamming twenty-five cents into the talk machine, drumming the numbers frantically.

"Hello?" Brooke answered.

"Pretty there?" Abdullah asked.

"Yeah, hold on," Brooke replied.

"Yo, Ab! Where you at?" Pretty inquired in a hyper tone.

"I'm by the riverside hospital," Abdullah revealed.

"Don't go around the way, Sami is riding around with the Jakes. Wayne, Hitman, and JC said she came through 2-4 with Sully in the gray Lumina. Dat bitch ain't playing, she rode through 2-2 too. Ant, Munch, South, Pookie, Stink, Piper, Little Joe all saw her. The heat is on!" Pretty said soberly.

"Damn! Dat no-good whore is probably running her mouth to them people about me," Abdullah said worriedly.

"Damn right she is. Ab, you're her connect. She ain't riding around with the police for nothing. Dat bitch is snitching," Pretty fired back.

"I'm getting ready to get the fuck out of Delaware, fuck dat! I ain't going back to jail. I ain't, fuck dat shit," Abdullah said firmly.

"I got a line on some cell phones and .380s fresh out of the box. Ab, I need a heater," Pretty said plainly.

"Pretty, grab me a phone. I got you when I see you, all right? Them .380s jam too much, fuck it, snatch one up for me, you never got enough burners," Abdullah said hurriedly.

The following night in West Chester, Pennsylvania, around ten something, Abdullah stood at a telephone booth.

"Ab, you is hot, you made the papers again. They said they gonna book you for them murders out Claymont. Yo! I rapped with Eugene Maurer. He said he would take care of you. He said he could get you off scot-free," Pretty relayed, pushing a '95 bluish gray Saab 9005 through the streets of Chester County, resting his mobile phone against his ear.

"It's no need for no mouthpiece, I'm not going back. I'm not turning myself in," Abdullah proclaimed, noticing Pretty pulling up.

Promptly, Abdullah disconnected the line, making his way to his friend Pretty.

Abdullah climbed into Pretty's SAAB.

"You all right?" Pretty inquired with concern in his voice, as he handed Abdullah a mobile phone followed by a chrome .380 semiautomatic.

Abdullah let out a sigh. "I don't got no choice. I gotta be all right, it is what it is," he said gazing at the chrome firearm he clutched.

"How you get caught up in dat shit?" Pretty pried.

"Dog, dat's the same thing I keep asking myself. I don't know how Sami could be a witness. Dat shit happen before I even knew the bitch, and I didn't tell dat bitch shit 'cuz I didn't do it, and if I did do it, best believe I wouldn't tell her shit. I wouldn't tell nobody, dat would go to the grave with me, believe dat," Abdullah said dryly. "I need you to go by my mommom's. Nah chill, the Jakes is probably jocking the crib, don't go by there.

"Monifah was crying. She told me to tell you she loves you. Listen, you can't keep driving the Lex, they gonna be looking for it," Pretty said calmly.

"I know, dat's why I need you to take me up Harrisburg, so I can lay low," Abdullah replied.

*****

A month later, in the dead of the night, Abdullah crept back into the nation's first state in a '83 white Cadillac Seville, sailing into

Pretty's middle-class neighborhood, eventually coming upon Pretty's driveway.

Abdullah stepped into Pretty's house where he immediately shook the hand of his longtime friend, embracing him warmly.

"Where Monifah at?" Abdullah questioned with dread leaping from his voice, as he scanned the living room for his girlfriend.

Pretty hung his head. "Ab," he paused, sighing. "Monifah got in a car accident tonight. She's in the hospital, but don't worry, she's alright, she just had to stay the night for observation."

"I wanna see her man. What hospital is she in? I need to see her, I gotta be there for her," Abdullah rambled emotionally and hysterically.

"Ab, think, calm down. Ab, you know you can't go to the hospital. Monifah's moms and pops and peoples are there... Ab, she's pregnant," Pretty replied.

In astonishment, Abdullah smiled ear to ear. "Yeah," he said.

"She'll be over tomorrow. Why don't you stay the night? You know she wants to see you," Pretty said solemnly.

"I'll lay my head here tonight, but I gotta keep moving. I can't stay in the same spot too long. Tomorrow night, I'm out, I'ma jet down South Carolina," Abdullah proclaimed, flopping onto the couch that decorated the living room.

"I'm kick it with you tomorrow," Pretty said, turning on his heels, exiting the living room.

Simultaneously, Abdullah drew a 9mm and chrome .380 semi-automatic from his waistband, placing the firearms onto a coffee table that sat in front of the couch he occupied. Then he reached down into his pants pocket, retrieving a fresh bottle of Hennessy. Energetically, Abdullah smacked the bottom of the bottle before twisting the lid off, gulping the liquor. Abdullah leaned over the coffee table, finger-tapping the button to the boom box. Power 99's "Quiet storm invaded the room while Abdullah leaped off the couch, making his way to the light switch, hitting the lever, transforming the lightness of the room to darkness.

As Blackstreet's "Before I Let You Go" blared from the boom box, Abdullah reverted to the couch, throwing the whiskey down his throat.

Before Abdullah eased into the kitchen, Aaron Hall's "When You Need Me," Sade's "Kiss of Life," Patti Labelle's, "If You Only Knew," Miki Howard's, "Love Under New Management," and Phyllis Hyman's "You Just Don't Know," flowed from the quiet storm.

Abdullah pulled open the refrigerator door. As Abdullah surveyed the ice box, he felt eyes digging into his back. In that instant, Abdullah spun around to find a very pregnant Brooke behind the dagger-like eyes. Slowly, Brooke made her way to Abdullah while she intensely gazed into his eyes.

"Damn, Brooke, you shining like a motherfucker, you hear me?" Abdullah crowed.

"Thank you," Brooke replied, flaunting a smiled.

"Can I touch your stomach?" Abdullah asked.

Brooke simply nodded yes.

Timidly, Abdullah touched Brooke's belly, placing his ear against her stomach, looking up at her. A sudden sadness immersed into Abdullah's being as he stood up peering into the windows of Brooke's eyes.

Meanwhile, Rose Royce's, "Wishing on a Star" traveled from the living room, easing its way into the kitchen.

"How are you?" Abdullah inquired.

"I'm fine," Brooke fired back.

"Are you taking care of my baby?" Abdullah said with sincerity in his voice.

"Of course... Ab, what do you think would happen if Pretty found out about us?"

"What do you mean by dat, Brooke?" Pretty queried upon entering the kitchen where Abdullah and Brooke stood looking on in shock as if they got caught with their hands in the cookie jar while the spinners' "Love Don't Love Nobody" hung in the backdrop.

"Pretty, it's not what it looks like or sounds like. Let me explain. You know I love you, right?"

"It ain't nuffin to explain," Pretty barked as his eyes held fire, forming tears.

Immediately, Pretty reached into his pants pocket, swiftly removing a chrome .380. As Pretty leveled the pistol at Abdullah and

Brooke, his face took on a wicked look. It was a facial expression that Abdullah and Brooke had never seen before. It was the look of an out-of-time, unstable madman, the glare of repugnancy.

"Pretty, baby, please, listen," Brooke whined sorrowfully while her eyes grew misty.

"I just wanna know one thing. Is dat my baby in your belly?" Pretty roared, carefully searching Brooke's eyes, trembling, afraid of what the answer would be.

Brooke swallowed hard. "It's yours, it's your baby," she said cautiously.

Abruptly, in a fit of rage, Pretty cocked the shiny lethal weapon, firing a round into the kitchen floor. Silently, Abdullah stood watching as his and Brooke's secret unraveled.

"Brooke, just keep it real with me. We can get through this, we can work it out, but you gotta be real with me. Who's the baby's dad?" Pretty said pathetically, narrowing the shiny firearm on Brooke while his hand fidgeted.

"It's Abdullah, he's my baby's daddy. I'm sorry, please forgive me. Please, Pretty, please. I didn't mean for this to happen," Brooke exclaimed regretfully, while the tears violently stormed from her eyes. "It just happened."

"No! No, no, no, no, no! This can't be. No!" Pretty yelled at the top of his lungs, savagely beating the .380 semiautomatic against his chest in despair, fighting back the tears that managed to fall from his eyes.

Pop! Pretty unleashed a slug in to Brooke's heart.

Horrified, Brooke stared hard and long at Pretty, before collapsing face-first onto the kitchen floor.

"You don't got nuffin' to say? Where your heart at now? Huh?" Pretty scoffed, turning the pistol on Abdullah.

"Nigga, I ain't gonna bow down to you. I ain't gonna beg you not to murder me. Knock me off, do what you gotta do, dog," Abdullah replied coldly as he took a deep breath, preparing to die.

Pop! Pop! Abdullah caught two hot bullets in his chest. Still on his feet, staggering, Abdullah desperately tried to reach for his 9mm and .380 caliber.

Just as Abdullah realized that he had left his lethal weapons on the coffee table another slug struck him in the chest, this time dropping him in the middle of the kitchen floor.

With his life slipping away fast, Abdullah lay on his back in the kitchen floor as blood squirted out of his mouth and the holes in his chest.

Bug eyed, Pretty dropped the firearm as if it was flaming hot, as if it was up in a blaze of fire. And with that, Pretty frantically hustled over to Brooke, flipping her from off her stomach, burying her in his arms while his tears raced down his face.

"Brooke, I love you! Come back! Come back! Come back! Come back! Come back to me! You can't leave me! Noooo!" Pretty howled regretfully while he vigorously shook the breathless Brooke.

Pretty sprang to his feet, scanning the kitchen, viewing the bleakness that decorated the kitchen, the dead bodies of Abdullah and Brooke, the kitchen walls and floors red with their blood. Nervously, Pretty paced back and forth. Then suddenly sirens blared out. The sirens screams drew closer and closer and grew louder and louder while Pretty stood in the kitchen contemplating on what to do next.

Pretty rushed into the living room as Jodeci's "Cry for You" pumped. He peered out of the window surveying the middle-class neighborhood for any law enforcement.

Not seeing a single badge, Pretty left the window to be greeted by Abdullah's 9mm that rested on the coffee table.

Without any hesitation, Pretty seized the lethal weapon as the sirens drew closer and louder. Pretty darted back into the kitchen. Crying uncontrollably, Pretty placed the firearm against his temple and slowly squeezed the trigger.

Pop! the bullet entered Pretty's brain, killing him instantly.

*****

"Brian Fairfax pulled a .380 caliber handgun on his pregnant girlfriend Brooke Collins, shooting her once in the chest, killing her. Then he shot his longtime friend Abdullah Saladin three times in the chest, mortally wounding him, before committing suicide and shooting himself in the head."

"The police said the shootings stemmed from a love triangle that apparently ended fatal. Ironically Abdullah Saladin was involved in another love triangle in which he was suspected of killing Trisha Fennedy. Investigators also said Abdullah Saladin killed Jax Davis, Trisha Fennedy's boyfriend, so he could embark in a romantic relationship with Trisha Fennedy while he was dating her best friend, Ebony Tatts. When Abdullah Saladin and Ebony Tatts's relationship soured due to his love affair with Trisha Fennedy, Ebony Tatts relayed to Abdullah Saladin that Trisha Fennedy was unfaithful, and that's when Abdullah Saladin snapped, brutally murdering Trisha Fennedy."

Mesmerized by the jaw-dropping news, Ebony turned the television volume up while her eyes bulged, intently observing the idiot box.

"Murder she wrote, I got away with murder, ain't that a bitch? Sorry Trish, I had to kill you, I couldn't let you win and be all happy. I couldn't let you win and be all happy. I couldn't, life isn't fair. I hope to God that you're rotting in hell, Trish, you backstabbing hussy," Ebony uttered to herself, plagued with scorn.

"Little Abdullah, come here," Ebony summoned her son, who was in the next room, who was the miniature version of Abdullah, as she still gazed at the television.

Several weeks later, on a sunny day, the singing Sami came out of hiding. Sami sat on the red-brick steps of an apartment building near the corner of West Twenty-Seventh Street, along with Joan, Regan, Candy, and Anitra. In a huddle by the street sign of Twenty-Seventh Street stood Rennie Rox, June, Beave, Shan, Twan, D-Nice, and Little John.

"Dat's crazy. What happened to Abdullah and them, huh?" Joan said, plucking the ash off the Newport cigarette she clutched.

"I know," Sami replied.

"Sami, on some real shit, do you think Abdullah really offed Jax and the girl Trish?" Joan questioned, inhaling the Newport cigarette.

"Honestly, no. I don't think he did it. We never talk about it either," Sami fired back.

"What do you mean y'all never talk about it? The papers and news said he confessed to you," Joan said with confusion in her voice.

"Bitch, I lied. He never said nuffin to me about Jax and the girl Trish. What, you don't know? Dat was my get-out-of-jail free card, shiiiiiiiit! Abdullah was hot, they wanted him for dat, I just helped them put the icing on the cake," Sami crowed.

"I thought Abdullah was your boy," Joan said in disbelief, slightly shaking her head.

"He was, but I can't do no time," Sami retorted.

Three days later, in the still of the night near the corner of West 27 Street, on the red-bricked stoop idled Sami and Joan. The two friends conversed underneath the streetlights that gleamed onto the pavement.

"I'll be back. I'm gonna cop some trees from Shan and them, they're up Twans," Joan proclaimed, hopping up from the steps, gradually blending into the darkness.

Moments later, as Sami sat by her lonesome, waiting for her friend to return with some marijuana, a mysterious figure emerged from out of the black of the night.

Slowly and slyly, the mysterious figure crept toward the unaware Sami. Meanwhile, from across the street from Sami lurked Joan behind a parked automobile inconspicuously, watching the mysterious figure move in on Sami, toeing up the opposite end of the red-bricked step.

Once the sole figure reached the top of the steps, the individual whipped out a knife, while Sami sat nonchalantly. Within a blink of an eye the mysterious figure roped their elbow around Sami's neck.

Desperately, Sami tried to fight off her attacker, but before she knew it her throat was slashed ear to ear. Sami's blood leaped out of her neck, spilling onto her clothes and the red-bricked steps. Fiercely, the mysterious figure kicked Sami down the steps, tossing a tiny piece of paper over her body. Evilly and heartlessly, Joan smiled as Sami's assailant dashed away into the night, making a clean and smooth getaway.

With a matter of minutes, Detective Ortiz and Detective Pitt arrived at the murder scene that was infested with badges. The two homicide detectives lifted the yellow tape and made their way to Sami's inanimate body. Sami laid on the pavement in her blood, on her back with a tiny piece of paper by her side.

In grief, Detective Ortiz and Detective Pitt stared at the emptiness in Sami's eyes. And with that, Detective Pitt pulled out a set of rubber gloves, settling them over his hands, kneeling, grabbing the tiny piece of paper.

As Detective Pitt stood straight up, he read the tiny piece of paper: "Stop snitchin'! If you can't stand the Heat stay the fuck out of the kitchen! Ha, Ha, Ha, Ha, Ha, Ha, Ha, Ha, Ha."

The End

About the Author

Chauncy Starling is a former death row inmate, who found passion for writing books while waiting his day to be executed in prison. During his time, he developed ways to help the youth and became an activist. Mr. Starling witnessed countless young men, just turning eighteen years of age, coming in and out of the prison system. Chauncy knew he was innocent and prayed to Allah (GOD) five times a day that if he ever opened the doors for him to see the light of day again, he would live right, leave the street life alone, and be the husband and father his wife and children needed for him to be.

To a great man.

Jeremy, I'm truly thankful
for everything you have done
for me!

Chris Stevens